BY HOOK OR BY BOOK
The Charmed Inn Mysteries Book 1
Misty Simon

Cover Art Design by: Kelly Moran/Rowan Prose Publishing
Photo Credit: Adobe Images/Deposit Photos
First Edition
ISBN: 978-1-961967-49-6
Rowan Prose Publishing, LLC
www.RowanProsePublishing.com
Published in the United States of America

Chapter 1

They called him Cheezy Rider—and with good cause.

I stood at the wide front window of the Charmed Inn with a cup of coffee in hand. I watched my great uncle toddling around the corner onto Chestnut Street, pedaling steadily on his old Beach Comber. The picture he made was something to behold. His bright orange vest perfectly matched the small caution flag waving from a tall pole attached to the back of the bike. His silver bullet helmet matched his thinning silver hair peeking out from underneath. But nothing matched his teal and red-flowered Hawaiian shirt.

His legs, covered in khakis, pumped away as he came up the block waving to anyone who happened to be on the short street in our small town on the shore of the Susquehanna River. The bicycle had a big wire basket on the front that he filled with a box of donuts from Delilah's Donuts every day, a place that had been in the same family for seventy-five years, like so many other businesses here. Those donuts were heading right for my work and then right to my hips. But I had never said no to pastry, and I wasn't going to start today. In fact, I needed the pick-me-up. Things were busy at the inn, with everyone checking in for the writers' extended working weekend, and sugar was always welcome. The staff wouldn't say no, either.

"I'm going to take a break," I said to my Aunt Hellen as I passed her in the hallway leading to the dining room. She was technically my great aunt, and she could keep things moving for a few minutes while I stepped out into the beautiful April afternoon sunshine. What I really wanted to say was that I was trying not to break, but that wouldn't be good for business. It had been one heck of a morning already, and I needed a moment to collect myself in the downtime before the festivities really began. Donuts were a great distraction, even if my erstwhile uncle did bring them every day.

"All righty, Ms. Mighty!" Aunt Hellen yelled back. This highly respected tasseomancer and seance-leader had a set of lungs that should never be allowed near a microphone. "I just finished having tea with Owen, so I'm free if you want to go on your walk, too. His phone rang in the middle of our tea, and it must have been important because he hightailed it out the door after making an excuse." She situated herself behind the desk and placed her hands on the computer screen like it might fly away if she didn't keep it locked down. "Hey, one thing before you go."

I held steady, waiting for the inevitable question. My life seemed to be filled with questions.

"What kind of afternoon do you think we're going to have? Should I restock the printer?"

Showing my teeth in what should have been a smile, I flipped open the book I held in my other hand, shaking my head at the ridiculousness of it all. Why, oh why, did I have to have this particular book with me? And why was my aunt always trying to force me to use my "gift"? I had no real power to do anything, just predict the future or get guidance from the text. Sometimes it was right, sometimes not. Either way, it was not high-powered magic in the least.

While poking my finger at the text, I said, "No need to stock the printer, but be prepared to deal with many irritations." There's nothing like trying to give a vague answer to a mundane question when the page you opened to was a spicy-hot scene between the hero and heroine in a recently released romance novel.

"I could have told you that. You have to try harder if you want to own your power, Roxanne Gleason. This is not a game." Peering at me over her bifocals, she twitched the classic "Mom finger" in my general direction and then tsked.

I resisted the urge to roll my eyes, but only because I knew it wouldn't do me any good. It would probably get me a lecture, and I didn't have time for that today. Plus, those donuts were calling my name.

"Yes, Aunt Hellen. Sorry, Aunt Hellen."

"Cheeky," she said under her breath, but I still heard it and smiled.

"Is Owen's nephew here yet?"

"No, Owen said he had to back out at the last minute, so we have a free room if we need it."

I sighed because as much as I liked Andrew, that was one less eccentric I'd have to deal with. Owen was a character all on his own, but he knew when to rein it in, Andrew not so much. Plus, his room would still get paid for even if he wasn't going to use it.

"Okay, thanks for letting me know. Keep an eye out for Paddy McGruver," I said. "He hasn't checked in yet, and sometimes he likes to come in the back door to avoid what he assumes are the paparazzi."

"Oh my, Paddy's coming in today? Will he be here all four days?" Aunt Hellen smoothed down the front of her shirt over what she jokingly called her shelf since it pretty much caught any crumbs she dropped while eating. She then pulled her peach cardigan closed over her stomach.

"Yes, and yes. Try to keep your hands to yourself this time. You read tea leaves, not rumps. No one is falling for that I'm-a-rumpologist-bit, no matter how hard you try to sell it."

With that, I walked out the door and left her to primp and prime herself for one of the more problematic creatives who was going to be here for four whole days. Well, not quite four, since it was more like seventy-two total hours from check-in to check-out. But who was counting?

With ten of the writers showcasing their intelligence and posturing over who had the best book and which classes were not to be missed, it would be enough time for me to need a vacation afterward.

The hotel hosted this event every year, but this was my first as the owner of this fine establishment. I had been told to give myself the seven days following the event to only host boring people, so I could rest, relax, and restore my faith in down-to-earth people. I had taken the advice since it had come from the previous owner, my grandfather. We would have guests checking in on Sunday after everyone left, but there wouldn't be a pen and paper or laptop in sight as far as the guest list went. I had made sure of it.

Uncle Vince was racking his bike at the side of the building and removing his helmet when I stepped out onto the wide veranda that encircled the inn. I looked forward to his visits and had for all the years he'd been in my life. I wasn't sure exactly how far away on my dad's family tree he was, just that he was there and always had been.

He was like a beacon in the middle of the day, everyone stopping as they strolled along the sidewalks to say hi and ask about his health. It kept him busy until I could reach him, which worked in my favor. As long as he didn't give away any of my donuts.

"I see you got two boxes this time," I said as I approached the old man in his loud get-up.

"Roxy, my love, my dove, how are we on this fine afternoon?" His smile was far cheekier than anything I had ever sported, and I immediately wondered what he was up to. It was almost never good. Or rather, it usually was good for someone but almost never good for me.

"What are you hiding?"

He slapped his hand to his chest and feigned hurt. "I would never -"

"You do. Always," I shot back, but a smile was trying to come out on my lips that I did not want to give in to. If I indulged him, he always had to see exactly how far he could take it.

"I'm offended."

"Only because I'm catching you before you can even begin. Hand over the donuts, and I might be able to see my way to just watching for any missteps instead of thwarting you before you even get started."

At first, he looked defeated, but I knew for a fact that was a lie. He'd just figure out a different way to get around me. It was a game he liked to play, and since he was an uncle and someone who had watched over me since I was a toddler, I knew, and so did he, that I had a weak spot for him and his antics. As long as they didn't hurt anyone.

Sure enough, that smile popped back out on his face. As I knew it would.

"I saw you in my scrying bowl this morning."

Ack, that was the last thing I wanted him to say. I would have preferred almost anything else, even the practical jokes he sometimes liked to indulge in. He wasn't very good at them, but I laughed, even if it was just a big fake spider on my porch. His visions were some of my biggest fears, though. Or it might be better to say his visions had brought about many of my stumbles in life.

"Keep it to yourself," I said, sticking my hand in the donut box and quickly picking a cinnamon sugar delight to cram into my mouth.

"No, no, I promise this is a good one. There's not a bad thought or dark anything involved. Promise!"

I shook my head at him, and he harrumphed. He could make noises all he wanted, but I wasn't giving in. He could, of course, tell me even if I didn't want to hear it, and he probably would, eventually, but for the moment, I was going to enjoy my donut and forget that whatever he had seen in his clairvoyant wanderings would probably bring me some kind of trouble. It always did.

The cinnamon sugary goodness was enough to bring me back to my normal operating level. This weekend was going to be fine. Three, almost four, days was always a quick stint with this many people, and it didn't matter if they were all creatives and some of them were off kilter. It would be fine. I had a great staff and a lot of wonderful help, and everything was planned down to the last folded napkin. I'd be fine.

"You're going to see someone new this weekend who will change your whole life and make you bloom!" Vince spit the words out rapid-fire, like a three-year-old holding on to a secret he just couldn't keep anymore. My little sister used to do that years ago, and I'd clap my hands over my ears. Unfortunately, with a book in one hand and the rest of the donut in the other, I didn't have any hands free to keep his words out of my ears.

And once they were in my ears, they had a much better chance of coming true. Dang it!

"What exactly did you see?" I asked, grabbing another donut because I deserved two.

Uncle Vince shrugged and used a deli sheet to get his own Boston Cream donut out of the box. He took his time closing the box and then placed it on the step next to him before eyeing the donut and turning it around to see which part he wanted to bite first. Once he found the right spot, he brought it to his mouth and took a big chunk out with his teeth.

I was going to scream bloody murder in ten seconds.

"Good stuff," he said after he chewed and chewed and then swallowed. He eyed the donut again, and I grabbed his wrist with one second to spare.

"Don't you dare. Tell me what you saw, or your donut goes in the bushes for the birds."

"I don't think birds are supposed to eat cream, Roxy. It's probably very bad for their digestive systems."

I growled, and he snickered.

"Fine, fine, fine. I saw a swirl of pink and blue intertwine to make a purple mist that floated out over the water and ignited a patch of beautiful roses in the middle of the river. The roses were deep red and antique, but they sparkled with dew that was both new and from a rainstorm that had passed earlier in the day. When I looked closer, the red was a twining of pink and deep burgundy."

"And from that, you got that I'm going to meet someone who's going to change my life?"

"Yes. Well, you'll see someone new. I didn't get a bead on if you'll meet them." He took another bite of the donut before I could stop him. Not that I was going to since I was still trying to figure out the symbolism of the mists, the flowers, and the dew.

I wasn't good at this kind of thing. Besides being a clairvoyant, Uncle Vince could cast spells that hit hard and fast. But he hadn't done one in years because they came with too high a price to his life. But at least he could do something, unlike me.

"Well, maybe I'll meet some person this year at the conference who will make my life much easier and do the books for me correctly instead of me trying to muddle my way through." Math and I were not friends. Words, yes, and someday I'd like them to work for me instead of me always working for them, but that was a totally different subject.

"Could be." But he didn't sound convinced. "Are you taking your walk today? I could come with you if you want to talk some things out. Do you have your speech ready to give this evening at dinner for your writer people?"

"Yes, I used my grandfather's, so it's pretty much the same as every year."

"And they love it every year, so don't disrespect it. This is a big weekend for you. It'll be great."

"And apparently change my life." I shot him a side-eye, and he just laughed.

"I'll take the donuts into Hellen, and you can go on your walk. I'll make sure she shares them with the rest of the crew."

He got up from the stairs with a groan and smiled at me as he dusted off his pants and straightened his collar. He'd had a crush on my aunt for years, but she'd never given him more than an almost friendly glance. My mother, who was Hellen's niece, had told me before my parents left on a trip around the country that the whole thing was not something I'd want to get involved with, and I trusted her.

I left my coffee cup on a side table on the veranda, along with the steamy romance novel, and tucked my hands into the pockets of my skirt as I took the four steps down to the sidewalk. We had one of the only remaining ferry launches on the Susquehanna River. And soon enough, cars would be waiting in line down at the bank to get across the river on the historic vessel when it opened back up next month. But for now, it was a beautiful place to wander along the grassy green and stare out over the water as I girded myself for the coming days.

It wasn't that there was any one person who would be in attendance that was a pain by themselves. They were all very nice for the most part. A bunch of older gentlemen and women who'd been coming here for years. They met to discuss the industry, took classes from people they'd flown in to discuss craft topics, and wrote and shared critiques. They ate every meal together and generally tended to try to one-up each other throughout the entire time. But it really was all in good fun.

So, it was going to be a big to-do, and a good one. But I still needed this walk, or my watch would yell at me for not taking enough steps.

Strolling down the hill from the inn, I kept an eye on traffic, while also allowing the slight spring breeze to ruffle my red hair. I was being a total drama queen, and I knew it, so I shook off my mood and quickened my step as I neared the path that ran along the river. I waved to Mrs. Lincoln, who was out sweeping her porch, and then to Ralph as he delivered the mail to the row of homes fronting the water. I was aiming for the bridge that crossed a small tributary, then I'd turn back around and head to the inn to check in more people before having to deliver that speech and get the whole event rolling.

The path veered away from the water, and there I met Dean as he emerged from one of the ferry sheds. Dean, who I might have secretly harbored a crush on when we'd first met, but I'd talked myself out of that, and now we were just best buds. It was the only way I could be around him without doing something stupid to impress him. Don't judge.

"Hey there, Roxy, you bringing the light? Are your glees on?" Dean Manchester wiped his big, strong hand on a rag as he walked toward me, making fun of my last name, Gleason. His painter pants hung a little low on his tight waist, and his chest filled out his t-shirt and hoody in a very nice way. Lordy, maybe I hadn't quite managed to kill the crush. I needed to stop thinking like that.

He was the resident handyman around town and had become one of my best friends over the last six months after he'd fixed a few things at the inn, and we'd hung out for days on end. He also thought he was funny when he was playing with words. The jury was still out on that one.

"Always teasing me about my last name. You still chesting the man?" Because the ferry was beached for the season, I figured he was cleaning the shed to get ready for next month when it would be back in the water.

He groaned, as he always did, and I laughed, as I always did. If he wanted to play with last names, then his was perfect for messing with. Bring me a ridiculous question and get a ridiculous response, Dean Manchester.

"What are you up to today?" I asked.

"Getting things ready for the season. Everyone checked in for the conference?"

"Well, everyone except Paddy."

"Oh, I bet Hellen is primping as we speak."

"You'd win that bet." In my peripheral vision, I saw someone sitting on the deck of the ferry. And that someone would get in so much trouble if anyone caught him there. It wasn't only very bad manners, but it was actually against the law. I walked over, dragging Dean with me, when I realized it was Owen from the inn, sitting in his bold purple suit, vest, and bow tie. Why'd he come down here?

I picked up speed, hoping to get to Owen before anyone else saw him. Like Mrs. Lincoln, who took great joy in talking with the police department and called once because a bird wouldn't leave her laundry alone on the clothesline she'd hung in the backyard. According to her report, the bird kept staring at her, and she didn't like it. So, she'd called because she'd wanted it arrested.

I didn't doubt for even a second that she'd have Owen in the back of a police car within a heartbeat of looking over this way.

"Owen, you have to get down from there. Right now, please. Come on." I looked around to see if any curtains had twitched or if anyone had come out of their houses to spy on what was happening. I stopped below him and reached up to place a hand on his knee, and he didn't even acknowledge that I'd spoken.

I looked up into his eyes and realized they were vacant. Glancing down at his chest, I did not see it rise or fall, and dread hit me hard right as he toppled to his side without pause.

He was dead.

Uh-oh.

Chapter 2

I was a reader. I had been from the time I was little. I liked every kind of book imaginable to some degree. Since my "gift" involved using text to get predictions, the printed word had been a part of my life for as long as I could remember.

And yes, I'd read every Nancy Drew and cozy mystery novel out there, along with thrillers, police procedurals, traditional mysteries, and noir.

So, I very slowly backed away from the corpse and immediately called 911, signaling Dean over to stand near the body. I knew what happened to people in stories who tried to move a dead body or immediately started searching for what happened to end the person's life. I was not going to be one of those people. I did not have time to go to jail or even the police station for questioning. Plus, I knew nothing. And I would say that a thousand times if I had to.

I glanced around to see if any curtains were twitching again because I did not want any more company out here.

Shirleen at the station answered my call, and I gave her a brief rundown while my mind tried to block how horrible this was, not only for Owen but also for the weekend itself.

Dean came up next to me and put his hand on my shoulder. The warm weight made me stop for a minute and sigh. Okay, I could do this.

"What happened?" Dean asked quietly.

"I think he came out here and died. He'd just had tea with my Aunt Hellen. I know when he left, but why is he on the ferry? She only said he left their tea to take a call. Did you see him earlier?"

"No, I've been in the maintenance shed for the last few hours tinkering with the fans for next month's launch. What do you think happened?"

Sirens blared as the police, fire trucks, and an ambulance came screaming down the hill and screeched to a halt at the curb next to the ferry. Dean and I stayed back as the EMTs checked for a pulse. The cops looked around. The one I had really hoped not to see emerged from his car, and I pulled Dean in front of me.

"Gah! Norm is here. Why did they have to send him? Couldn't it have been anyone but him?"

Dean chuckled at me for a second, and I tugged on the back of his shirt.

"I don't get what you have against each other, but I'm pretty sure he has more important things to do right now than give you a hard time about finding a man who died out in the open with no obvious injuries. He's old, Roxy. It could have just been his time."

Speaking of time, I glanced at my watch and realized I had to get back to the inn and get ready for the speech and tell the guests one of their own was gone.

"Can you stay and answer any questions?" I asked, backing away. "Let someone other than Norm know where I am if they need me."

"Of course. You might want to at least check in and tell them that yourself, so no one gets any stupid ideas, though."

Always the corrector. But he was right.

I moved off to the left to throw my donut paper away when there was a commotion over by the ferry. Norm started yelling loudly enough to make the ducks on the river flutter down to the next clump of beached tree branches.

"Don't you leave, Roxanne Gleason. Don't you dare leave. This here is a murder."

That stopped me in my tracks and had me turning around. Norm was storming toward me, and I so wished I had a book to find out what this particular prediction of an outcome would be. Although, I had far more trouble with my own questions than when someone asked me something. And he wasn't asking, he was demanding.

Dean stepped right into Norm's path, and as much as I was sure Norm wanted to go around him, Dean wasn't going to let him. While Dean was built like a tank, Norm was more gangly. I would have thought he'd grow out of that after we'd graduated high school, but he hadn't.

I couldn't get my thoughts to go right in my head and stood locked in place. Owen was dead. Had someone killed him? Does this mean it might not have been a natural death because of age or some illness?

But how had he been killed? Why had I not seen anything? And how did Norm know that when standing with him for less time than I had? Was it something obvious I had missed?

Those thoughts got me moving, along with the fact Norm had started growling at Dean to get out of his way. No hands had been thrown just yet, and I was pretty sure Norm would be able to hold himself in check in his civic duty, but I couldn't make that assumption for Dean. And I didn't want my friend to get in trouble.

"I'm not going anywhere," I said. "I was just over at the trash. What is your problem?"

"My problem, Ms. Gleason, is that I have a dead body, and as far as I know, you were the last one to touch him and the first one to see him dead. So, I have questions."

Was he insinuating I had something to do with this? I could feel my hackles bristling and wished so hard for the ability to zap him with some kind of magic that did something. But that wouldn't have been good for me either because there was the pesky rule of things coming back on you threefold.

I did not ask the question about what he thought I might know because I was not going to open a sealed Pandora's box if he hadn't meant it that way. Instead, I walked back over to him and Dean and stood slightly behind Dean, who was not only built like a tank, but he was also much taller than almost my five-foot, one. I doubted Norm would try to reach for me, but I wasn't taking chances.

"What could you possibly think I know?" I asked as firmly as possible but without an edge to my voice. There was a history here, and I wasn't going to exacerbate it, but I also wasn't stupid.

Norm ran a hand over the top of his thinning brown hair and blew out a breath. He stuck his hands on his hips and then planted his feet wide. If he was looking to intimidate, he was going to have to do better. I lived with Aunt Hellen. No one intimidated me.

"He was dead when you approached him?"

"Yes." I had watched enough TV to know to keep my answers short and directed at whatever he was asking.

"Did you know he was dead when you approached him?'

"No."

"Did you touch him?"

"Yes."

"Was he cold to the touch?"

"No."

Norm tugged on his hair as Dean took my hand in his. He gave it a squeeze and then dropped it. I would have been fine if he'd continued holding it and given me warmth in a situation that was seriously going off-course into frigid.

"I'm not going to yell. I swear I'm not going to yell." Norm blew out a heavy breath.

I couldn't tell if he was talking to me or himself, so I waited as technicians began arriving at the scene and scurrying around Owen. Poor soul.

"I need more information than what you're giving me," he finally said. "One-word answers are not going to help. And you and I might not be the best of friends, but I would think you'd want to help someone who *was* your friend."

He was almost being nice to me, and I tried to overlook who he was as a person and focus on who he was as a professional.

He squinted at me. "Unless you were the one who killed him."

Well, that went right out the door.

Drawing in a deep breath, I settled myself before speaking. "Look, Norm, I have no idea what happened. I came down here for a walk, I met up with Dean coming out of the shed, and I saw Owen sitting on the deck of the ferry. I thought he'd get in trouble if Mrs. Lincoln called you all up at the station to report a crime because if she wants birds arrested, I'm pretty sure she wouldn't hesitate to tattle on someone resting on a boat. Which he should not have been doing, so I was going to tell him to get down before anyone saw him, and then we wouldn't have had any issues at all. But when I lightly touched his knee to get his attention, his eyes were vacant, and it didn't look like his chest was rising and falling with breath. Then he fell over and didn't move, so I stepped back and called 911 immediately while asking Dean to stay with the body."

I probably took a breath in there somewhere, but it didn't feel like it. And Norm was just staring at me after I closed my mouth. I hoped he'd gotten all that because I didn't know if I could or wanted to repeat it. What I really wanted to do was go back to the inn to process this before I had to tell anyone what had happened, or at least the part where Owen was dead. I didn't want to think about his death not having been a natural thing or even an accident.

"Well, that's quite the story," he said. "I guess we'll have to see if it makes sense when we process the scene."

As soon as he closed his mouth, I was on fire inside. "You have got to be kidding me. Why would I kill one of my guests and put him on a ferry and then come by and just happen to discover him? That makes absolutely no sense." I stamped my foot on the ground and then felt like a toddler. "I called 911, Norm. Why wouldn't I just let someone else find him?"

"Okay then. How about this? Maybe that's what your boyfriend here did. He says he was in the shed and saw you walk by, so he came out to say hi, and then you found the deceased. Don't you think that's a little weird? Why didn't he see the dead guy walk by?"

Now Dean was the one growling, but low and with far more vibration and intent than Norm had before. I put a hand on his arm.

"Look," I said again. "I've lived here for a very long time, and I'm aware that you're probably freaking out inside with a population of about 2,500 and very few unexplained deaths, much less murders in the town, but don't be an idiot."

Norm bristled. Fine with me. I wasn't telling any lies.

"Did Dean see him earlier in the day?" I asked. "Did he come out of the shed at all until he saw me? Did you ask him any of those questions?"

"I hadn't gotten around to that yet." Norm's demeanor didn't change in the least, even as he pretty much admitted he was being the idiot I'd warned him against being a few seconds ago.

"How do you even know Owen's been murdered? He could have just climbed up on the deck to take a short rest, and his heart gave out. I didn't see any knives, and he's not bloody, so how do you know it wasn't just that his heart gave out on him?"

"Perhaps because his bow tie is so tight around his neck that it cut off his breathing and circulation. He was strangled with his bow tie, Roxanne. You didn't see that when you 'lightly touched' his knee to get his attention? When you realized that his eyes were dead, and he wasn't breathing?" Norm's eyes narrowed.

"I - I didn't see that."

"Interesting." He took out a notepad and pencil to write something on the page. What I wouldn't have given to get my hands on that particular book.

"You can leave now, but be available for questioning. And no avoiding me. I know you have that ridiculous writers' thing this weekend that always seems to have me running around, putting out small fires, but this is big. The last thing I need is more complications or to be ghosted."

"Of course," I said, feeling sick to my stomach. This was worse than just letting everyone know one of their own had left this mortal world. This was a murder. Someone had taken Owen's life. Had they killed him and then left him on the deck of the ferry for someone to find? Or had they killed him in broad daylight right on the ferry itself, less than an hour after he'd left the inn? I needed a book, and I needed it now.

I took off for the inn as fast as I could manage. In heels and my more businessy outfit of a skirt and oversized sweater that wasn't exactly fast, I was trucking to the best of my ability while also trying to not break myself. I had a lot to think about and do, and I didn't know where to start.

I was so deep in thought that I missed anyone walking behind me and jumped when someone grabbed my arm. I was ready to come out swinging but stopped myself when I realized it was Dean.

"There's no fire," he said. "It's going to be okay. They can't actually believe it was you. Norm is probably just trying to get you to react, and that's exactly what you're doing. Slow down."

Because even though he had a hold of my arm, I was still trucking. "I don't care what he's trying to do. This is horrible, and I can't even begin to know how this is going to affect everyone who's at the inn right now. What on earth happened? Why would someone do that to an old man? And with his bow tie? Do they even make those things strong enough to withstand being used as a garrote?"

That last question was kind of ridiculous, but it had popped into my mind. Apparently, I was currently unable to have any kind of filter to keep it from popping out of my mouth. I needed to get myself under control. I could not be in this kind of state when I arrived at the inn.

So, I stopped, shook Dean's hand off my arm, and bent over at the waist with my hands on my knees. I took several deep breaths until I felt more centered and made myself blank out my brain. It wasn't easy since it felt like a frenzy of bats trying to get out of an attic at dusk up there, but it had to be done.

Dean, bless him, stood by my side but didn't try to do anything except just be there. That was what I needed more than anything, and I'd thank him later. After I got myself together.

I stood back up and rearranged my sweater from where it had fallen forward. "Okay, this is not the end of the world. This is not something I had anything to do with, and no matter what Norm says, I did nothing wrong. So, he won't be able to prove it was me if I did nothing wrong." Of course, that was when the cascade of true crime podcasts I listened to came streaming into my head with all those people who had been in jail for years, no matter how much they protested their innocence. And even after the evidence was proven false. I was going to be sick.

No, no, I wasn't. I was going to be strong, and I was going to take this whole thing in stride and count on the fact Norm was not the only person on the force. And even if he didn't like me, I still truly believed he would want to find the real killer, not just pin it on me because we'd had a run-in years ago that obviously he couldn't get over.

"I'm going to go back to the inn. I'll wait for dinner to pull everyone together and make my speech, but preface it by saying there was an unfortunate incident down by the river. I can do this."

"Of course, you can. And I'll be here if you need me. I don't only chest men, you know."

I laughed before I could stop myself. Fortunately, it did not turn into a sob. I could do this, and I would do this. And maybe if I did it right, I wouldn't be charged with anything I didn't do.

I took the last three blocks to the inn at a more leisurely pace. My brain was still churning, and Dean was still by my side, but I felt more confident and more settled. For that, I was grateful.

"How am I going to tell everyone Owen died under horrible circumstances?" I asked Dean as we rounded the last corner to the veranda.

"Well, I don't think I'd start off wording it quite like that."

"Of course, I won't, but the thought is there."

"What makes you think they don't already know?" Dean pointed at the large window I'd stood in earlier, thinking about donuts. There was a significant gathering in the lobby of about twenty people, and they were all chattering away excitedly.

"They could all just be getting ready for dinner," I said.

Dean glanced at his watch. "At one p.m.? I don't think so."

He was right, of course. Darn it!

Everyone was so focused on someone in the middle of the room that they didn't notice us coming up the porch stairs. The murmur of conversation came through the window as we approached the double front doors.

Paddy McGruver brought his voice to full volume, and I could hear him loud and clear, even through the wood and glass.

"Quiet down, everyone," he bellowed.

Dean and I stepped into the vestibule as quietly as possible and stood off to the side to avoid notice. I wanted to hear what Paddy had to say before announcing myself.

"As the most prolific and decorated author, as well as the only *true* mystery writer in residence at this time, I can tell you there will be many clues and red herrings we might find in this untimely death. None of us are qualified to really investigate, though, not even me, so I suggest we keep our opinions and speculations amongst ourselves. And let the police do their work. If they ask you a question, keep the answers to a minimum. We can, of course, discuss this throughout our stay, but let's keep out of the professionals' way as best we can."

Aunt Hellen fluttered her lashes at him and clasped her hands in front of her chest like she was a damsel in distress just now seeing the knight, or maybe she more resembled an overzealous fan girl. That fit a little better, especially with her slightly wild hair and her disheveled cardigan.

Either was not what I needed at the moment, but I had a feeling I wasn't going to be able to do anything to snap her out of it.

How did Paddy know already?

Did he have something to do with the death? More importantly, was I going to look at every single person in this place as a suspect instead of a guest? That was going to be awkward. I despised awkward.

Chapter 3

I did not want awkward for over seventy-two hours, and I did not want to think everyone was capable of killing someone. Most likely, there was a simple explanation. Maybe they'd just seen the trucks racing through town, and someone had gotten a tip. Most likely, though, Paddy had probably talked with someone right after the sirens sounded. I wouldn't put it past him to have been on the fringe of the crime scene and able to get some information and then hustle back here to share it as the resident expert on all things murder. It ran with who he was.

Aunt Hellen looked like she was going to be useless since she was hanging on his every word. The man could have been reciting his grocery list, and she would have been just as rapt.

"Psst. Aunt Hellen." I peeked around the archway to see if I could get her attention before announcing my presence.

She completely ignored me. She was so wrapped up in Paddy that I could have lobbed a grenade at her, and she probably would have just sidestepped it and kept fawning.

Yet another reason why I had kind of dreaded this weekend. Or not exactly dread it but had been loath to do it? Yeah, that was better. I loathed this weekend because it often ended with hurt feelings or posturing. And my aunt was always on Paddy's side, no matter how rude he could be, like now.

"Listen, everyone, no one has a voice like mine, the presence of me, the intelligence I display at every turn, from the porch to the bedroom. I am a scholar of life, a lover of the fine things in my sphere, and an influence to be reckoned with. I tell you again, Owen was murdered because he was not willing to play the games that someone had foisted upon him, and therefore, he had to go."

What the heck was he talking about? I motioned again for Aunt Hellen to join me, and again she ignored me. So, this time, I yanked her by the arm around the corner, and she didn't make a sound. She was a professional and understood the rules about making a scene more than almost anyone.

"I need to talk with everyone, but I also need Paddy to not interrupt me. Can you please do something about him?" I asked her.

"Oh, I could think of a few things I'd like to do with him -" She trailed off with a mischievous smile on her face that not only made me want to groan but also maybe puke a little.

"He's a menace, not that you'll ever see that. But I need to talk to everyone, and I can't do that with the man who thinks he is God's answer to everyone and everything talking incessantly."

She shrugged. "I have no idea how to stop him. Maybe you'll just have to barge in with a stark warning and talk right over him. I can usher him into the sitting room for a drink if necessary to show him that not everyone is rude enough to not take his words as gospel."

I really hoped she was kidding, and it did look as if she might be purposefully laying it on thick. She palmed a locket at her throat and widened her smile. "Time to go grab the goat by his horns."

"Everyone, everyone!" She steam-rolled her way into the room as if on important business. "Roxy is in need of your attention."

I had hoped for something a little more subtle, but I'd take what I could get. I left Dean in the vestibule and stepped out to address the crowd. "I'm so sorry to confirm that Owen is indeed deceased. I found him at the ferry launch and thought he was just taking a rest, but unfortunately, it was more permanent than that. I don't have any information or answers yet, but tonight's dinner will also be in honor of him and his wonderful contributions to this society."

There were a few grumbles. Not everyone liked Owen as I did, but they could just keep their opinions to themselves.

The questions started about two seconds later. They were flying through the air like a bevy of butterflies had been released from a net. I couldn't catch most of them, but I didn't have to.

"As I said, I do not know anything more at this point, but I am certain the cops will be by to do some interviews, so if you know anything, I would share it with them. Firsthand knowledge is usually best so as not to muddy up the wheels of justice." Keep your theories and storytelling to yourself, I thought, but there was nothing I could do about what they told any interviewer.

I excused myself after that, but no one even seemed to notice that I left. Fine with me. Paddy immediately took up grandstanding again, but it was just more of the same of what he'd already said.

Thankfully, Dean was still around the corner in the vestibule. I whisked by him as if I didn't see him, hoping to make it to the next turn in the hallway, where he wouldn't know which direction I took.

I needed a plan, and I needed a book. But I couldn't do the book thing with Dean around because he didn't know about my "gift" thing. And I couldn't count on Hellen because, well, see my last thought on that. Crap.

But he followed me, and he was far faster than I would have given him credit for.

I wasn't escaping him, so he'd have to be ignored after all. We'd known each other for a few months, and he'd done several jobs around the inn. We had a blast when we were together and had gone out with groups of friends to live shows at the restaurant down the road or the brewery in the next town over. I liked talking to him, and I enjoyed having him around. He was the closest thing I'd had to a best friend in a long time. I didn't want to mess that up by having to ask him to believe, even for a second, that witchy stuff was not only possible but real.

Yes, people knew about Hellen and her tea leaf reading and seance leading. They also knew about my Uncle Vince's ability to dream of what could come and a little about my grandfather's ability to persuade. But it was always passed off as parlor tricks. They called them magicians and giggled. We were just a family of clowns who'd chosen to set down permanent stakes in the town on the river for our carnival of oddities.

But how would I get around that without outing the truth?

I'd done it before when I was younger, so I used an oldie but goodie.

"Hey, while they're all occupied blabbering amongst themselves, do you think you could come into the library so we can talk about what to say to the police?" I asked as casually as possible.

He shrugged. "Sure. I have a feeling I'm not going to be allowed near the shed for the rest of the day, regardless. And I don't have any other jobs until tomorrow. Plus, it might be a good idea to put our heads together to see what we each know, if anything."

He was so practical, that Dean, and believe me when I said in an inn filled with creatives and people like my aunt, I welcomed that with some pretty heavy appreciation.

We eased down one of the hallways that split off to the common rooms available to anyone who was staying at the inn. We had a dining room, an exercise room for those ambitious souls who didn't want just to relax, a massage room where you could get a heated stone massage or a facial, and we had a game room complete with not only a pool table but also a dart board and table-top shuffleboard.

This group tended to use a couple of the rooms, but the one at the end was the pinnacle of delight for them. It was a two-story conservatory set up as a library with old literature and newer fiction. We had a small section of reference books, but with the internet, most people stayed away from them. The whole room was dotted with small clusters of chairs, some leather and some so comfy and soft I'd sometimes find people half-asleep in them and have to encourage them to head up to their room.

And because it was two stories, and I was a sucker for *Beauty and the Beast*, one entire wall had a rolling ladder. I had to admit that when I'd first had it installed, I'd tried to push off and make it carry me from one side to another. I would not, however, admit what a mess I'd made. We'd just leave it as it didn't work and was never tried again.

Since everyone was in the lobby, that meant no one was there. Now I just had to figure out how to get a book, get Dean to ask me questions, and then read the answers without looking like I was ignoring him to read when I was asking. Completely doable.

Of course, I was totally lying to myself, and this was going to be tough.

But I had an idea. I climbed up that ladder and very cautiously pulled myself along the shelving while Dean took a chair below me.

It wasn't until I was ten feet in the air that I remembered this might not have been my best idea with a skirt on. So, without explaining myself, I climbed back down and then walked to the staircase on the left and sedately climbed up the steps to the second-floor balcony that ringed the library on the other three sides. I'd pretend I was looking for something while he sat in the chair facing the other way. This would work. It had to.

I ran my hand over the spines. Dean was saying something, but I figured it was probably just rehashing what we'd already gone over. I needed to find a book that was willing to talk to me. None of them called to me at all as I trailed my fingers over the spines. I was in the women's fiction section. Maybe I needed to go to the mystery section?

I wandered to the right along the wooden railing.

"Are you listening to me at all? I just asked you like three questions, and all I'm getting is some kind of humming that isn't a song but sounds like I should know it."

I glanced over the railing and stared at him. "I'm humming?" I never hummed. Why would he hear humming?

"Something is humming. But now that I'm not talking, it seems like it's more coming from over there." He pointed to his right under the ladder.

"It's probably just the electricity in this old place." I was pretty sure I was lying, but I couldn't tell him that.

"How handy that I'm a handyman. I can take a look."

"No, no, that's okay. I'm sure it's fine." Actually, what I was afraid of was the book I needed was over in that exact spot, and it was transmitting to him as a hum.

I had to think fast. "Hey, before we get into talking about what we know and don't, would you mind going to the kitchen and getting us some tea or hot chocolate or something? I can text Glennis and ask her to get a tray together if you don't mind picking it up?"

He didn't immediately agree, so I felt the need to over-explain myself as I always did in situations like these. Or really any situation.

"I'd really appreciate it if you'd do that for us. I'm afraid if I go out there and the guests see me, I won't be able to escape all their questions. Or God forbid, more suppositions and stories of how it could have happened."

He grabbed the arms of the chair and pushed to rise from the old leather. "I was getting up. You don't have to explain yourself to me. Just ask, and I'll do whatever you need me to. No justification needed."

And he was out the door. Okay then.

As he walked out, my errant black cat, Moose, short for Mustafa, came strolling in. "You are not supposed to be here, sir," I said, but I still reached down to pet him by stroking my hand from the back of his head to his tail, just the way he liked it. He meowed at me, and I realized that my time was running short before Dean would be back. I would deal with Moose later. "Stay here. Do not wander into the main inn."

Leaving him on the balcony, I scampered down the stairs. There really wasn't another word for it. And I immediately went to the area Dean had gestured to. I had a few minutes before he'd be back, but I wanted the book right now so I could figure out how to hide it and still use it.

Not for the first time, I wished that I could use any text. It should be just anything that was a book. My official title was bibliomancer, so I should have been able to use any "biblio" as far as I was concerned.

I could pull up an e-book and could use it and hide it like I was doing something very important in my planner or calendar or sending a message to the staff. Anything but putting my finger on a paper page and having to read the line that usually had nothing to do with what it would say to me. Usually, the words themselves were indicative of the message, but the message needed to be pulled from the words. It was hard to explain, and that was why I was happy not to be able to share it with anyone, as in I literally could not tell a soul that was not in my family. But a computer or any kind of techy screen would have been nice.

Although, I guess I should just be happy I didn't have to read some ancient tome from the Middle Ages and cart it around in a satchel in case I needed it and not sneeze from the musty smell.

It was the little things.

I felt the pull from five feet away. No matter how many times this happened, it was always a hit or miss as to if I'd know what to do with it once I touched it. Sometimes, I'd pick up the wrong book. This one, though, was hard to miss. It was sparkling. That was new. And it was making so much color it looked like confetti was being thrown around with wild abandon.

As soon as I touched it, the book and the glitter settled down, and I hoped the humming would, too. It almost floated out from the shelf and stuck to my hand, but that had to be my imagination. Moose meowed above me. I ignored him.

Of course, the book I had was a how-to book on gardening. Why not? I suppose I needed it to make any kind of idea bloom on how to deal with this horrible situation. The universe had a sense of humor, after all.

I flipped through the pages to see if there were any messages for me without a question. That had only happened once before, but I kept hoping it would happen again or be a new level of my power.

Not today.

Dean came back in, followed closely by Glennis and a rolling cart of not only hot chocolate but also donuts and croissants with ham and cheese and a veggie tray. What were we doing? Having a picnic?

"Just wanted to see if you had come up with any kind of theory," Glennis said as she parked the trolley and started moving things to the small cafe table between two chairs with velvet heart-shaped backs. "The staff is afraid they'll have to talk to the police, and all seven of them keep asking if we think you've done it. Of course, the answer is no, but they're really afraid the cops will try to stick it to you, love."

Well, crap. I forgot I had a book in hand when I went to make a fist and dropped the book instead. It flapped open, and though I could see the black type, what really caught my eye was the letters dancing above the book in gold sparkly dust. That had never happened before. The words couldn't have been more clear to see but less clear to understand: *Welcome to the game that's afoot, Sherlock. Prepare to be run through the gauntlet. Get your magnifying glass out and keep your sidekick close.*

Chapter 4

What game? Was I Sherlock? What gauntlet? Who on Earth was my sidekick? I had never had letters float off the page or sparkle golden before, and I'd rarely had such a strangely cryptic message given to me by a book. Sometimes, they might be hard to decipher, or someone asked about their kitchen appliances while I happened to be holding a horror novel that would show me something about a tortuous machine, and I would have to decipher even though I really didn't mean to.

But this was totally different, and I had no idea what to do with it.

Beyond that, it had just occurred to me that I might not be the only one able to see the glowing letters. That could have been why Moose was meowing from the balcony but didn't come down to investigate. I moved to shield the book from Glennis and Dean, hoping I had been quick enough to hide what was happening. However, at the same time, it also occurred to me that I might want to know what they could see.

All these questions and just so few answers.

But one thing I did know was that I wasn't going to get any more answers here, and I needed to get back to the conference-goers to find out what they knew if anything. Maybe some of their theories would help since they told stories for a living and might be able to help with how this plot might have unfolded. Why not use them to my fullest advantage? Especially if the police were going to try in any way to pin anything on me or Dean.

After a brief conversation, where I made excuses about leaving, I left Dean and the small impromptu picnic in the library, along with Moose, and took the book with me to see if it had anything more to say. I had every intention of coming right back once I checked in with the guests to see if they had any information I might need. I would have to put my cat back in my rooms, too, but Dean had said he was happy to stay with him for the moment.

I opened the book again once I was out in the hallway. Running my fingers over a few pages, I got nothing, not even the usual pinpointed sentence that normally answered my question. Crap.

I'd have to try later. Right now, I had more concrete things to do.

Fortunately, my Aunt Hellen was the first person I came across. She was leaning against the doorframe leading into the living room, where everyone had migrated. Maybe standing around in the lobby had gotten old. Paddy was still waxing eloquent, and she was running the locket at her throat back and forth along the chain.

"Anything new here?" I asked at her shoulder. She was a robust woman and towered over me, but I made up for the height difference with an oversized personality. Or at least that's what she told me whenever I said I wished I was taller.

"Nothing other than Paddy being a genius with the theories and speculation. He's so dreamy."

This coming from my normally very straight-laced and practical aunt. One of the few normal people I had in my family.

Well, that was until she got around a cute older man, especially Paddy. I didn't understand the fascination, but I needed her here and her help on this one. Dreamy was not going to fit the situation unless he was the one who'd offed Owen.

"I would really appreciate it if you'd help me out," I said as I tapped her on the shoulder to get her to turn to face me.

"And I would really appreciate it if you would respect that I am currently not on the payroll and, therefore, can do almost anything I want, especially if that means fawning over one of the most intelligent men I've met."

She needed to get out more. That's all I was saying.

"You've met many intelligent men who don't tell bogus stories and beef themselves up to always be something they actually aren't."

"It's not bogus," she grumbled and seemed to sulk a bit.

"Believe what you want, but I know the truth. I've read his work. It's good, but it's not that good."

She harrumphed and then grabbed the locket at her throat, moving the charm back and forth over the chain.

"Is that new?" I had never seen it before, but I'd noticed her playing with it a couple of times now. She was a big shopper, and packages arrived for her all the time, but I hadn't seen this until now.

"Oh, yes." She blushed and ducked her head. "It's from a secret admirer. I know who I'd like that to be, but I'm going to hold off on guessing and hope that the giver is willing to tell me who he is."

"A secret admirer? How do you know that?" A little strange, but I guess it's not totally off the charts.

"It's what the note said." She sighed this time. "They left it for me at the front desk in an adorable velvet box with a tag attached. 'To Hellen, the lovely reason it is good to be alive. Please wear this so that I might admire the way it sparkles at your neck.' It was signed Your Secret Admirer." She giggled. "Isn't that lovely?"

"Um, yeah, sure." Actually, it was lovely and fun in the middle of this yuckiness, but I'd have to appreciate that later. "Listen, I need your help to see what we can do and if we have any information," I whispered because I didn't want to call any attention to us when I needed to be discreet.

I lifted the book to test if she could see the floating letters. I had tucked my thumb between the pages to mark my spot, and when I opened it back up, I hoped the letters would be right there glowing and dancing. But they weren't. Had I imagined it the first time?

"Oh, that's lovely," she said, moving the charm back and forth faster like she was unaware she was doing it. Finally, she let it go to trace the trajectory through the air where the sparkling gold letters had finally begun to float again.

"So, you can see them?" I asked. "It's not just me? Why couldn't I see them when I opened the book last time?"

She bit her lip and dipped her finger through the word Sherlock, then closed her eyes and breathed in and out like she was doing very concentrated yoga. I did not have time for all this.

"Aunt Hellen! I need help here, not mysticism. Please."

That seemed to snap her out of what she was doing and put her back on track with what I actually needed.

"Yes, I can see the letters." She cleared her throat. "I don't think there's anyone else who would be able to see them, at least no one who was non-magical. You can't see them now?"

I turned the page back around, so I was looking at it straight on, and they appeared. Okay, well, that made me feel a little better. "Do you know why they're sparkling like that instead of just allowing me to read a sentence on the page and extrapolate the meaning? That's how I normally do things, and this is very different. I don't know if I like that feeling right after Owen was found."

"Perhaps you've grown your gift, my dear. I tell you all the time that if you'd use it more, it would help you more. Even gifts don't like to be ignored." She lowered her voice and pushed her hand over the book like she was covering its ears. "I'll tell you a little secret, they're like dogs. The more you train the gift, the easier it is to use. It's a great trick."

The book jumped in my hand, and I wondered if that was my talent telling me it was unhappy with my aunt's assessment? I'd never had that happen before, either, so I felt like this might be a new level also. This was the very last thing I needed in the middle of a big weekend. Almost worse than a murder, but not quite.

Speaking of which, it was time to figure out who knew what, if anything, and then take it to Norm so he could leave us alone.

"If I could have everyone's attention." I'd been waiting until Paddy took a breath to launch into his next topic so that it didn't sound like I was interrupting him even though I was very much interrupting him. But he didn't take a break and appeared to just be getting on a roll, so I had to jump in when he took a breath.

Paddy opened his mouth wide, then clamped it shut when I shot him a look.

I had been prepared to do much more, but I was fine with him taking the cue I was throwing to him just this once.

"The police are going to want to talk to everyone and anyone, especially any of you who had contact with Owen before he left. Did anyone see him actually walk out the door?"

"I know he got a phone call while he was having tea with Hellen." Erma Flava didn't talk much, so when she did, I tended to listen.

"Right, the phone call." I looked at my aunt. "Did you hear anything sitting across from him?"

"No, the phone rang in his jacket pocket. He took it out, looked at the screen, and then excused himself. I didn't see him again after that."

"And no one else saw him?" I kept trying to think of any other questions I could ask to generate conversation but was coming up with nothing. Where did all my armchair sleuthing go? I usually knew whodunnit minutes after a TV show or book started, and I was almost never wrong. But all the tricks in my mind were missing in action right now.

Everyone in the room shook their heads in the negative, and I wasn't sure where to go next.

"I sure hope they don't think any of us did it. Killing someone on the page is vastly different from killing someone in real life," Jenny Walden said.

"Of course it is, dear. No one thinks otherwise," Paddy said, and my aunt gusted out a lusty sigh.

I did not need this right now. I needed answers and to figure out why the letters were glowing golden off the page. I had a book in my room that detailed what powers people like me had used throughout the ages. I made a mental note to check that out once I had a few minutes to myself. I could do it when I dropped Moose back in my area at the inn. He preferred being in my sitting room but would also often hang out in my bedroom too. At this point, I just needed to follow what I'd been told by those golden letters and wait to research later.

"Well, let me know if you come up with anything," I said lamely, then left the room.

I needed to get people thinking and apparently figure out who the book and Universe thought my sidekick was.

As if to answer my question, I came across my Uncle Vince snacking in the kitchen with the staff. He put his hand over an apple turnover as soon as I walked through the swinging door. Like I wouldn't be able to see what he was eating.

I rolled my eyes. "I've told you before, I'm fine with you taking stuff from the dessert cabinet if needed."

"Right, but these are brand new, and I wasn't sure if that was also allowed." His cheeky smile was something that often brightened my day, and so were the donuts he brought. Not at the moment, though, since my mind was too full of unanswered questions and concerns.

"It's fine, just don't eat them all. I'm sure Glennis knows exactly how many we're supposed to have for the guests, and I know she always makes extra. So, as long as I have enough to go around out in the dining room, I'm fine with you eating one of the extras. Emphasis on one. Glennis makes them for the staff too because who wants to spend all their time making the perfect dessert but not being able to then partake in it?"

"He's not exactly helping," Glennis said as she turned from the stove to point a spatula at the old man. "He's in here getting everyone hyped up about a possible serial killer in the area."

Nothing could have stopped me from shooting poison darts at him with my eyes. "Seriously?"

He harrumphed. "Well, it's not out of the realm of possibilities. This could be the beginning of a type of spree. Perhaps something happened to spark the delusion, and Owen was only the first?"

Clara, who was rarely sensitive to many things, and that's why I had her washing dishes, which she said was a godsend for her overactive hands and imagination, dropped a plate, and it shattered. The tears started immediately, and they weren't hers.

They were from Taylor, one of our newest hires. She'd been a favor to a friend, and I was happy to have her here, but any and everything seemed to set her off.

"Thanks, Uncle Vince."

He shrugged, finished the last of his turnover, and then scooted out of the kitchen through the back door. Glennis took Taylor by the hand and walked her over to the prep bar while Clara grabbed the broom and cleaned up the mess.

"Clara, when you're done, can you go grab Moose from Dean in the library and tell Dean we'll talk later?" She nodded, and so I turned to my next task. They seemed to be never-ending right now.

Since the kitchen staff had everything in hand as best as could be expected, I followed my uncle out to see where he went and to get a read on what he thought of the situation. He was in his seventies and spry and very smart, plus he had his finger on the pulse of the whole community. He might have some insights that I would need in order to keep things as in line as possible while the cops did their thing, and I tried to get our guests to do their own thing around the cop thing.

I finally caught up with him on the front porch, where he had stashed his bike.

"Where are you going?" I asked as he removed his helmet from the front wire basket.

"Oh, I'm sure there are all kinds of theories flying around over at the diner and probably the bar at this point, definitely the lunch counter at the mercantile."

Yes, we still had one of those. Sometimes, I thought the clock had stopped in the fifties once you crossed over into our little town.

"So, you're going to go eavesdrop on people and see what they have to say about the murder?"

He laughed to the point he had to hold his belly to keep from falling over. "I'm not going to eavesdrop. I'm going to include myself in every single one of those conversations. And then I'm going to go home and see if I can have a vision to find out who actually did it. Come on now, girl. You know me better than that."

I did know him better than that, and I should have thought of what his actual goal would be. He was even nosier than I was, and that was saying something. "All right then. Will you share whatever you find with me? I have a whole inn of people to protect, and I'm very concerned."

Leaning in, he dropped his voice to a whisper. "You should be concerned because I'm almost certain it was someone in your house right now, and if they did it once, they very well might do it again. You might want to keep a book in your hands at all times, my dear."

The door opened and closed behind me. Uncle Vince laughed again, loudly, as if he'd just told a dirty joke.

"Now, don't go telling your mother I told you that one, girl, or I'll get into trouble. But definitely do share it with your friends. That's the ultimate test of whether or not you have good people around you."

He hopped on his bike and toddled off much the same way he'd toddled in a few hours ago with donuts. I wished we could go back to that time and place before we had lost Owen and gained a murderer.

I waved him off, a little concerned with who I'd turn around and find. But it was Glennis.

"Everything okay in the kitchen now? I'm sorry you had to handle Taylor by yourself."

"Pshh, don't even worry about it. That's why you pay me the big bucks." She folded her aging hands at her waist, and I knew there was more, or she wouldn't have come out here, away from her favorite domain where she ruled the roost.

"I'm wondering if this weekend is going to make it absolutely necessary for a raise." I laughed but wasn't feeling very full of mirth at the moment.

"I'd never say no to one, but I don't think it will. We just have to keep our noses clean and our heads down and not get involved. I know you're not a big fan of Norm, but he does know what he's doing."

Did I want to wade into that one with his aunt? They weren't close as far as I knew, but he was still her family, and I tried not to mess with that if I could help it. "I'm sure he does to some extent, but this isn't a traffic violation or a kid trying to prove his tough side by robbing someone's pool shed in the backyard. This is murder, and I'm afraid we're just getting started."

"Well, just keep your eyes open and your mouth shut, and we should be fine. I promise."

Normally Glennis was able to get me to calm down and see the big picture when I was freaking out about a chipped teacup or sandwiches that looked too flat.

This time, she sounded ominous instead of helping toward calm. And that made me even more concerned that we were in for some serious shenanigans.

Chapter 5

Part of me wanted to take Glennis's advice and just stay out of the whole thing. But the other part of me, the bigger part, to be honest, wanted this solved. Especially if it was someone in my house like Uncle Vince seemed to think. Even more, especially if Norm really was going to try to pin it on me or Dean. My best friend did not need that kind of headache when I knew there was no way he'd ever be able to do something that horrible.

Why did this have to happen now? I'd already known the weekend was going to be rough with so many people and so many planned activities, but this could be beyond my wildest nightmare, and I had some doozies.

We only did a few events during the year because, normally, we operated as a true inn. Just having the rooms and serving food was enough for the small staff I had on hand. I'd brought in extras for this weekend because we'd be serving all meals and snacks and keeping the coffee hot and ready, tea too. I had not put murder in the schedule, and it was throwing me off my stride.

But that was nothing compared to entering the foyer and coming face to face with my grandfather. I kept the sigh in because it wouldn't do to let him know I was not prepared for him to be here. I should have known he wouldn't be able to stay away.

Benson Marks had been a detective in days gone by and still liked to do that from the armchair in his living room. His true position had been as a forensic accountant. But as far as he was concerned, he was the best of the best at anything having to do with the law, especially with bringing those to justice who broke it. I usually let him ramble on about all manner of things only because it was easier than trying to stop him. Today was not going to be a usual day, though.

"I don't have time, Poobah. I have so many things going on, and pre-dinner drinks are supposed to start in two hours." I glanced at my phone. "Ugh, less than two hours, and I have a houseful."

He nodded and stuck the pipe in his mouth that he hadn't smoked in twenty years. "Mmhmm, you also have other things happening in your houseful, and we need to get them moving in the right direction immediately, or it will sully our name and take you on roads you had no intention of going. My crystal ball told me I have to participate to keep you from a complete downfall."

I did my very best not to groan. Instead, I sighed slowly, like a balloon that had been pricked but not popped. "You haven't used a crystal ball in my entire lifetime."

"Fat lot you know." He grinned around the pipe, and it almost fell out of his mouth. He quickly righted it and then nodded his balding head. "We are all in on this one."

"There is no *we* and no *in*, all or otherwise. Go home, see what Bubby, your errant dachshund, is doing, and leave this whole thing to the police."

That got a laugh pretty close to Uncle Vince's but not quite so robust to have him holding his belly. I was surrounded by elderly people who thought they were hysterical, or maybe they thought I was hysterical. That was something to contemplate at a later date or even just a later time.

"See here, I know things, and things tell me we are going to have to at least help the cops, or they're going to ruin your whole thing here. I don't know what that means, but I did consult the spirits, and they said we have to help."

"You shouldn't be drinking this early in the day."

"So funny, that's what I told your mother you would be on the day you were born. So very funny. Who knew how right I would be? I'll tell you who. Me, I knew. Now, I also said you would have an amazing curiosity, and I know you want to look into this. If for nothing else than to solve it so you can get the rest of things done around here. So, let's stop arguing, and how about you listen to my proposition?"

It would not do me any good to try and fight him. He was many things, and one of those many things was incredibly tenacious. He'd pursued my grandmother for seven years before she'd agreed to even go on a date with him. Then he'd proposed to her thirteen times before she'd said yes. When she'd passed five years ago, I was certain he would follow her right into the grave, but he was still hanging on to this mortal plane, and I appreciated that. In all things, he was not a quitter.

"What is your idea? And I'll tell you if we can do it." I was making no promises and yet trying to keep an open mind.

"I think you might want to go check to make sure that Owen didn't take his teacup up to his room after having an afternoon sit down with Hellen. You know how people tend to forget they're not supposed to take things to their room, and you might just want to make sure he was following house rules."

"I'm positive he left it on the table since Aunt Hellen said he got a call, left the table, and went outside."

He stared at me, and the light blinked on in my head. A little late, but still, it blinked, and that counted for something.

"Poobah, there is no way that would fly. I shouldn't be in his room at all, just in case."

"Just in case, you should absolutely be in his room. In fact, I just now remembered he promised to return a walking stick I'd lent him two years ago, and I don't want the police to confiscate it in their search. That stick was very important to me, given to me by my grandmother. I would hate for it to end up in an evidence locker. Wouldn't you? You'll inherit it one day, so I need to secure your inheritance. I insist."

"You cannot be serious." But in the back of my mind, I was definitely entertaining his idea. I couldn't deny it. I wanted to see if anyone had rummaged through his room or maybe taken anything. I did have to protect my guests' privacy at all costs. It was part of the fee they paid for staying here. That was my story, and I would stick to it like crazy glue against Norm if I had to.

"One quick trip as long as we don't touch anything." I hoped I wasn't about to screw myself over this, but I also wanted to see if any of the books in his room could tell me anything. According to some legends, proximity to an event or a person involved in the event could occasionally shed light on the text I found, even without a question.

I couldn't believe I was actually going to do this, but that didn't stop me from taking the back stairs from the kitchen to the second floor after checking to make sure the police hadn't shown up yet.

If Norm truly thought Dean or I had done anything, then he was going to have a very big uphill battle to get that to stick. I'd see to it. And part of seeing to it would mean investigating on my own.

I went first and left Poobah to travel up the stairs behind me. If anything was at the top of the stairs, or if anyone was in Owen's room, I would have far more reason to be checking on it than my grandfather. He had owned this hotel until late last year, giving his whole family an amazing place to grow up. Not on the premises since he and my grandma had always maintained a separate residence. But we'd had Christmases here and picnics when the inn was empty, or nearly so. My grandfather would host a family reunion every year, and more than a handful of my cousins had gotten married here in the library or the backyard. My older sister had gotten married here, too. My younger sister might one day, but she was currently running around in Europe doing whatever it was you did in Europe. My grandfather had left the inn to me to run three months ago after he'd had a heart attack and had been given strict orders to calm down and slow down. I would have done it just for that reason, but really, more than anything, I loved it here.

But me running the place meant it would make far more sense for me to check on a room than my grandfather. That didn't mean he didn't try to bypass me in the hallway after we emerged from the painting at the top of the stairs hiding the door, but I stuck my arm out and held him back.

"No. Let me go first." I couldn't believe I actually had to say that after all the maneuvering I'd done to keep ahead of him.

"Fine, but make it quick."

This comes from the man who could take an hour to eat a side of bacon if he was in his storyteller mode.

"Back down there, Poobah. I've got a plan." I didn't really, but I was usually pretty good on the fly, so we'd go with that.

I very quietly knocked on the door marked with the number ten, sitting on a ferry. It had been the logo on these doors for over a hundred years. My great-aunt had painted them with a brush charmed by her husband's grandmother long ago, and somehow, the paint had never faded or flaked.

The quiet knock was because I wanted to be able to truthfully say I had tried to announce my presence before opening the door just in case anyone was in the room. But I heard nothing on the other side of the door, and when I opened it, the room was empty. A few cases were open on the bed, things were strewn over many of the available surfaces, and the closet door was ajar, but the room was empty of people.

"I don't remember Owen being this messy. He almost always unpacked and put everything away first thing so he could feel like he wasn't going anywhere for the next few days." Poobah pushed past me once he saw the coast was clear. "After we go through everything here, we should check out his car. There might be something there that would point us in the right direction."

"We don't need to be pointed in any direction. Anything we find should be handed directly over to the police, and then we wash our hands of it."

He scoffed because, of course, he did. I knew him well enough to know that was not going to go down well, but I still had to try.

"We can't mess things up, or we might make it impossible for them to catch the killer."

Another scoff. "And you really think Norm is going to be able to figure out the complexities of what happened to get Owen from a tea with Hellen to the dock after a phone call and then strangled with his own tie? You don't think he's going to go after the one man he's been jealous of for the last six months when all signs could point to Dean if he just follows that path and makes any evidence fit his prejudices?"

"Norm is jealous of Dean? He wanted the contract to clean the town and keep up the landscaping?"

Poobah rolled his eyes. If he scoffed again, I was going to push him out the door and lock it so he couldn't get back in.

"You have so much to learn, my girl, but we'll leave that alone for now so we can dig into what might be missing here. I don't remember this being what Owen's room usually looked like. In fact, he was always incredibly neat. So, I'm assuming someone was looking for something. Did he find it, though?" He stuck the pipe back in his mouth and stared into the distance.

If he had a duster and a deerstalker hat, I was certain he could have been mistaken for Sherlock himself. Was he my sidekick? I wasn't sure if I'd be able to have him that close that often. I adored him, but he could be a bit much sometimes.

"Don't touch anything," I said as he reached out for a sweater hanging off a fake ficus I'd put in the room because Owen liked plants and requested one every year, per Poobah. So, when I'd taken over the inn, I'd made sure to continue the tradition. But since I killed any plant before it could fully clear the front door, I'd made it fake and just pulled it out of storage in the attic the day before I knew Owen would be here.

Several of the branches appeared broken or at least bent in the wrong direction. How could all this destruction have happened, and yet I'd heard nothing? Yes, the place was big, but I would have thought someone would have heard something.

Poobah had taken the time to use my distraction to grab a cane Owen had often been seen with that was leaned up against the wall and started poking at things on the floor and the bed.

"What did I say?" I asked, the urgency in my voice sharp even though I kept the volume down.

"Pssh, this is my cane. I let him borrow it two years ago, and every time I asked for it back, he'd ditch me without answering."

I closed my eyes because that was not a good enough reason to move or touch anything. And now, I was going to have to explain why my grandfather's fingerprints would be on at least one item in here. If nothing else, I was certain Owen had not been bludgeoned to death because then that very cane could have been the weapon.

So many things, so many complications, so many bumps in the road, and we were only a handful of hours into the investigation. I kept feeling like I had definitely bitten off far more than I could chew.

That feeling only intensified when the door whipped open behind me, and Norm barked my name.

Chapter 6

Well, this had not been on my bingo card for the weekend. I closed my eyes before I turned around to address Norm. I needed a second to compose myself and not fly off the handle at him. Plus, it would not be a good thing to show him I was surprised or felt guilty for being in here. This was my hotel, my room, my establishment, and this was not where Owen was killed unless someone had strangled him here with his bow tie. Then, somehow managed to carry a dead body all the way through the inn, out the front door, and then down to the dock without a single person noticing something was wrong.

"Yes, Officer? What can I do for you?" I folded my hands at my waist like Glennis had, wishing desperately that I had a book in hand to give me concrete answers on how this was going to go. If I had a real talent, I'd be able to conjure something up to shield me from his view or make him forget he'd seen me. But I didn't have any talents like that, so I was just going to have to weather the storm on this one.

"Well -" He stopped there and adjusted his belt, then pulled at the collar of his uniform shirt.

I waited because I was not offering anything, no excuses, no information unless he asked for it, and even then, it would be as close to one-word answers as I could get.

"Well -"

You already said that. I thought, but didn't say it out loud. I just waited, and it made him antsier. Good.

"What are you doing in here?" He finally stopped fidgeting and stuck his hand on the gun in his holster.

"I wanted to check on Owen's room. I was going to lock it so no one would be able to get in before you and your crew do whatever it is you'd need to do after you investigated the actual crime scene." Oh, see, good on the fly!

He squinted at me, so I continued. "I wasn't expecting to come into a disaster, to be honest with you. Have you not sent anyone up here to look into what state his possessions were in yet?"

Poobah tsked and then moved the pipe from the left side of his mouth to the right while shaking his head in disappointment.

I knew that move well, and though it didn't work on me much anymore, it had a distinct effect on Norm.

He blew out a breath, grabbed the back of his neck while bowing his head, then lifted his gaze slowly and looked around the room. What was he thinking? I could make up a hundred different scenarios in a blink, but he appeared lost in the moment, if not lost in the whole situation.

"I was looking for you to let you know we're going to start interviewing people," he spat out.

"Of course, and if you need to get to that, we wouldn't want to keep you. As I said, I wasn't expecting to enter to find things all over the place. Perhaps whoever killed Owen also went through his room, though I don't know what they were looking for, and I'm not sure if they found it. I'll leave that to you."

I pulled Poobah by the elbow behind me as we skirted around Norm and headed directly for the front stairs. I wasn't going down the back ones the way I'd come up. It was time to get ready for the dinner and the welcome reception, though I didn't feel very welcoming at the moment.

Poobah grumbled as soon as we got to the landing and tried to tug against my hold, but I was having none of that.

"Come on. We have to get out of here."

Something thumped against the stairs hard enough to reverberate in my shoes, and I was horrified to see that he'd taken the cane with him.

"Oh no."

"Oh yes," he said and wiggled his eyebrows at me. "And don't tell me I should give it back or that I was wrong to take it. I don't need you to tell me what to do, so don't."

"You really should give it back."

"It's mine."

"It could be evidence, and you're going to make it worse if you don't give it back. If that's found anywhere near Dean at any point, even if he's standing near you and you leaned it against the wall, Norm could take it as something he stole out of the room. People have seen Owen with that cane for the last two years. It's distinctive." That was a bit of an understatement. It was ebony polished wood with a dragon head, and it hid a sword in the cane itself. Owen would pull it out and brandish it whenever he felt like it to show it off and threaten people jokingly. I guess if I was looking for a silver lining here, it could be at least Owen hadn't been stabbed.

"Lean it against the wall right now and leave it there."

"You can't make me."

"*Now*, Poobah. You should walk it back into them and say you took it because it's yours, but I think that might make things worse. Just lean it against the wall."

"Lean what against the wall?" Norm again. I would swear he was stalking me or at least us.

"Poobah saw his walking stick right outside Owen's door and took it with him, but I'm concerned it might be something you would want since Owen has had it for the last two years." That sounded so lame. And yet, I didn't have another answer, and it was just a tiny lie, not a huge one. Man, I hated this.

"Hand it over." Norm held out his hand. Poobah grumbled under his breath, but he did as he was asked.

"Traitor," he said in a near whisper. I ignored him.

"If that's all, then I'm heading down to my guests to see if we can salvage anything of the first day of this long weekend."

"Don't leave town, Roxy."

He had to be kidding. Or not very bright. Who even said that? Maybe he needed to stop watching too much television. "Did you not hear the part where I said I have a long weekend of activities? Where would I go? I run the place, and the place is full. If you need something, you know where to find me." I turned on my heel and hit the stairs at just below a run. Something about Norm had always bothered me, and I didn't like him any more now than I had throughout the years. But if he thought he was going to bully me or my guests, he had better gird his loins because I was going to aim where it would hurt the worst. His ego.

As I came into the drawing room, I put those thoughts aside and took in the twelve people before me. They were writers, editors, and readers who just had a lot of money and no real desire to write but they acted like it so they could keep their friend circle. Paddy was one of the few who actually had any publishing credits.

I'd known most of them my entire life. This was a yearly tradition, and this was the thirtieth year here. Some had been to every single one of these weekends, some had dropped out when life got to be too hectic, then came back when they missed the group too much to stay away. And some were newish. But I was familiar with every single one of them, and I just couldn't imagine any of them being a murderer.

Poobah put his hand on my elbow to stop me from entering the room.

"While you were thinking in the room, I poked around a little."

I sighed. Hopefully, he hadn't pocketed anything I wouldn't be able to explain away like I did the cane.

"Did Owen ask to use the safe in the cellar at all?" Poobah whispered.

"No." But why would he? Almost no one used that thing.

"He was supposed to bring a very special book this weekend, and a lot of people had hints of what it might be. He'd told me he was finally bringing it with him, but I didn't see it anywhere. I highly doubt he would have forgotten it. So where is it? Is that what the person was looking for? Did they find it?"

Those questions very much echoed my thoughts when we'd first entered Owen's room.

"What was the book?"

"It was that family diary he's talked about over the years. He finally found it, and it was the first half of some sort of treasure hunt. He was all about showing the thing off and having it judged by your antique book dealer. But I didn't see it. He sent me a picture of the case he carried it in, and that was there but not the book itself."

"Do you think he might have had it on him when he died at the boat dock?"

"I doubt that, but it might be something you'll have to tell Norm." He leaned against the wall, looking at me expectantly.

"You tell Norm. I don't know anything about the book, I've never seen it, and he said nothing to me about bringing it with him. You're the one with all the info. I'm pretty sure Norm would rather have a first-hand account than a second-hand one." At this point, I did not want to ever talk to Norm again if I didn't have to. In this situation, I definitely did not have to.

"I have a feeling he'd take it better from you now that you outed me as a thief with my own walking stick." With that, he walked into the room, all smiles and jovial small talk. He complimented Agatha Smalls' nails and Francine Metzger's bright and obnoxious shirt. He even talked to Paddy briefly, which was unusual. He kissed his daughter Hellen on the cheek and then poured himself a brandy before taking a seat in a lounge chair. And then the show was all up to me, and I wasn't sure I was prepared for how this was all going to go down. Why did life have to be this hard?

But at least everything was set up the way it was supposed to be. I counted on Glennis a lot to get everything where it was supposed to be and when it was supposed to be there. She never let me down. The punch bowl was set up, and a ring of skeleton head ice cubes floated in the bright red mix of juices and soda. She'd made a basket filled with pieces of bread and then used our small spring-colored leaf dishes to hold jams and hummus and butter as well as cream cheese. But her real masterpiece was the bookshelf filled with books she'd made of vegetables. Move over charcuterie boards, Glennis and her crew were on the case.

Each book spine was a row of different colored vegetables, and she'd even made a cat sitting at the base from black olives.

It reminded me of the cat I'd had when I was growing up, pure black, so gentle, and so sweet. I'd had him until I was eighteen, and when he'd died, I hadn't been able to bring myself to get a new one. I enjoyed Uncle Vince's kitty when I would go by his house, but I had enough to do without adding an animal on top of my list of things and people to care for. Or at least that was what I had told myself right before I brought Moose home.

Moose that I hoped was back in my room. I couldn't believe I had left him and Dean alone for so long, but at least Dean had the little picnic set up, and maybe he'd found a book he wanted to read. I was glad Clara had been available to tell him he could leave and take Moose to his bed.

Yes, I was fully aware I was going to be doing some intense apologizing once I finally got back to Dean.

Enough looking over the spread of food as if I hadn't been absolutely sure Glennis had done an amazing job. I was just procrastinating, and I knew it.

"Welcome, everyone." I turned to face them all with the food behind me. I didn't need a podium, and that was in the dining room anyway, which was being set up for dinner right now.

I cleared my throat. "We've had quite the start to our yearly get-together. I'm so sorry Owen is not here with us."

"How do you know he's not?" Frances popped out of her seat and began pacing along the thick rug. "How does anyone know where the spirit goes once it is released from its corporeal prison? He could be floating in the atmosphere right now, wondering why we're sitting around looking at bread horns when we could be out finding out who killed him."

"Officer Norm asked us not to do that," I said quietly but also firmly. For one, I could talk to my cousin and see if Owen actually was still hanging around because that was her talent. And two, if Frances started stomping around the house and the town, there was every reason to believe she would cause havoc. That was just what she did even without a murder to solve, and we all knew it.

I had to head her off as early as possible. I had a decision to make, though. Should I tell them I was going to look into the murder, and they could let me know if they heard anything? Or should I tell them all to stay out of it and let the police handle things because, of course, they would know how to do their job?

That last one was not going to fly, no matter how much I spun it. I'd done debate in high school, and while I could be incredibly persuasive when needed, even I would struggle with making that sound at all fathomable.

Although maybe I wasn't being fair to Norm and his fellow officers. Perhaps he really would know what he was doing and do it well, even if he had no experience with this.

Besides, it wasn't like I had any real-life experience with this, either. Although I did have all those books, I could tap into them if I'd tried harder, like Aunt Hellen said. And I had vast experience from listening to hour upon hour of true-crime shows. That sounded lame even to me, though.

Decisions, decisions.

Frances grabbed her coat from the stand in the hall, and I knew I had about one point two seconds to make a decision.

"I'm looking into this. And I'd really appreciate it if all of you would help me by staying here and throwing around ideas about what questions to ask and who to ask them of. I have plenty of ties to the community you wouldn't have, and asking the same person six times for the same information is not going to help anyone. Would you do that in your novels if you really wanted to find a killer?"

That seemed to stop everyone in their tracks. Frances sat back down on the couch, and even Paddy stopped waxing eloquent. I could be on to something here.

"If you all help me with the right questions or angles to look at, and we do find the killer, I would make absolutely certain the paper runs an article on the bravery and cunning of the writer's weekend posse who brought about justice. I'm sure that would do wonders when you're sending out queries or short story submissions. And it's far more likely to happen if we work together as one team, letting me ask and then bringing the information back here to be mulled over instead of a bunch of vigilantes showing up one after another with the same questions to the same person, who might decide to just not open their door or their mouth after the second time."

Their facial expressions would have been comical if I wasn't so intent on getting them to agree with me. Much contemplation was going on in those brains of theirs. I opened my mouth to further make my case when Poobah laid a hand on my forearm. "Don't sell it too far, or they'll feel like they're being told what to do. You gave them the bait. Now wait while they eat the hook, and then you can reel them in."

Chapter 7

I waited like my grandfather had asked me to. I tried very hard not to feel like I was watching a glacier creep across a plain over the course of the years it took to move one foot. It was in no way easy, but in the end, I was rewarded for my patience and for taking Poobah's advice. I'd never hear the end of that one.

"I think that is actually a brilliant idea, Roxy. In fact, I was just about to suggest it, but you cut me off before I could get the words out." Of course, that was Paddy talking and gesturing wildly with his scrawny arms.

No matter how much I wanted to correct him, because no way had he been about to say that, I instead graciously nodded briefly at him and then turned to the room in general.

"Okay, so I'm thinking we can use the drawing room as the congregation space. And I'd really encourage you all to continue to show up for the lectures we've set up and the professionals you've paid to have come here. We have every meal together, so we could talk then, but I can also get a suggestion box to put ideas into if something occurs to you between meals."

"Oh, this is like one of those murder mystery weekends now instead of the conference, but it's a real murder!" Erma clapped from her place on the biggest chair in the room. Her brown eyes twinkled, and you'd think she'd just been told she was getting her own pony for Christmas. I'd wanted one when I was ten, and Poobah offered to get it for me, but my mom had talked him out of it because I didn't tend to stick to things. I lost interest pretty quickly through the many years and many types of activities I'd tried from age three as a ballerina to age eighteen as a lacrosse player and the hundred things I did in between. But when the possibility of the pony had first been considered, I'd definitely clapped like that. Of course, I'd been ten and not sixty-five, but we all had our inner children riding shotgun for these kinds of things.

"So, it's settled. We'll discuss any new information at meals, and I'll have a box where you can put ideas if they come to you. If you just can't wait until the next meal to talk about it. And we will then hand everything over to the cops because I'm certain in the end they'll be able to be competent."

There was a chorus of groans from the amateur investigators' gallery, which was interrupted by a huge commotion that started behind me with crashing, banging, and a whole lot of swearing. I turned toward the steps, but I didn't get more than two feet closer before Norm came tumbling down the stairs, his arms waving and his mouth hurling obscenities like they were confetti.

He landed right at my feet and closed his eyes for a moment after looking out at the crowd before him.

Did I say competent? I was pretty sure I had...

I reached a hand down to help him up, but he pushed it away. He growled as he did it, but I didn't think it was directed toward me since he was looking back up the stairs, and I heard someone quietly say they were sorry and oops.

Yikes.

I was still keeping to my plan, though. No matter how much I did not like Norm as a person and the way he had just completely shown his incompetence instead of his competence, that didn't mean he wouldn't be able to solve a murder, even though he'd never solved one before.

I was very much trying to believe that.

Norm stood up and brushed off the front of his pants. He shook back his hair and then zeroed in on me. "I'm going to need you down at the station. I have questions, and you'd better have answers, or we're going to be having a very different conversation where you'd better make sure you look good in orange."

*In*competent!

What in the actual hell was he talking about? "I beg your pardon."

"You'll be begging me for a whole lot more than that if you aren't at the station in an hour."

"I have commitments and no information I haven't already given you. I can't do an hour." I was pretty sure he wasn't going to take that well, but he surprised me.

"I'm willing to let you get whatever moving that you need to handle here for your guests, and then you need to hustle down to the station first thing tomorrow morning. No delays." With that, he looked up the staircase again and then stomped out the front door.

I peeked around the banister and was surprised to find Micah Felderman standing at the top of the stairs with his face as red as one of those cherries I loved to put in my Shirley Temple. Micah was young. In fact, I had babysat him when I was twelve and he was four. He'd always been a good guy and helpful to the point of overwhelm. Was he still like that in the police force? Had he done or said something that had caused Norm to fall down the stairs?

I didn't feel comfortable asking him, so instead, I turned back to the big room of people and put on my best possible smile.

"Let's get dinner started, and then I guess I'm going to the police station. Maybe I can pick up a clue or two about what Norm knows."

A few people leaned their heads in together, and I desperately wished that I could have supersonic hearing instead of the ability to randomly pick out words on a page and have a fifty-fifty chance of being able to tell the future with any real accuracy.

Although, I also very much just wanted to sit down on the steps and drop my face into my hands and then probably cry but mostly scream.

I lifted my gaze and caught Aunt Hellen looking at me. She shook her head with a quick motion and then jerked her head back toward the kitchen. Once she saw me nod, she moved toward the kitchen door, expecting me to follow probably.

"All right, everyone, at this point, let's get the dinner hour started so I can go answer the police's questions before Norm decides to come drag me away in cuffs, even though I didn't do anything." I laughed derisively and was joined by several of the guests.

"So are the gloves off then to find out who really did this if Norm is going to be stupid enough to think you'd kill one of your guests for no good reason?" This came from Erma, who looked intrigued and also a little pale. She probably just needed dinner, and so did everyone else before they started complaining.

"Let's get into the dining room, and we'll see what we all know before I go and put myself at that guy's mercy." I waved everyone into the dining room and let them take their seats, designated by the beautiful little cards Glennis had made for the weekend. I told Poobah he could take my place, and he gladly dropped his rear end into my chair without another word.

Once they were milling around like they should be, looking for their names, I excused myself and took a leisurely stroll back out the door. As soon as I was out of their line of sight, I hustled the rest of the way to the kitchen. I could have gone in through the side door that was attached to the dining room. It would have been faster, but I didn't want to have to explain myself or have all those people standing with their ears pressed up against the door to see if they could hear anything.

Why did things have to be so complicated?

"Finally!" Aunt Hellen said when I made it through the door.

"Shhhh! They don't know I'm in here, and I'd really rather not talk in front of them until I know what's going to be said." I shook my head and then grabbed my right shoulder to pull some of the tension out with a stretch. The last thing I needed right now was to have my neck seized due to stress.

"You really think they don't know?" Glennis asked and then pointed the pokey end of her knife toward the black and white television screen hanging in the corner above the other door. While the writers had been milling around when I'd left, it appeared they all decided to stop within inches of the door opposite me as soon as I rounded that corner and thought they'd forget about me in the chaos of finding their seats. I was wrong. Although that really wasn't anything that new.

Glennis rolled her eyes, cranked open the walk-in freezer, shoved us through the doorway, and shut us both in.

"Do you think she'll let us out if we ask nicely?" I asked Aunt Hellen.

"Eventually. At least you have long sleeves on. I'm still in my spaghetti-strap shirt since I intended to put my cardigan back on right before all this happened. What exactly did happen?" she asked.

There was nowhere good to lean in here. Between the boxes of frozen vegetables and the trays of meat on wire racks, I was afraid of accidentally knocking everything over. At the same time, I was concerned that if a part of my flesh touched the frigid hardware, I'd get stuck like that kid in that Christmas movie with his tongue on the flagpole.

"I have no idea. I called the cops when I found Owen down on the ferry where it was dry-docked."

"And then?"

I shrugged. "The police came in and started looking around. I tried to walk away, but Norm practically ran at me and told me to wait and not leave town. As if I would." I rolled my eyes at that, but I was starting to freeze over and hoped my eyelashes wouldn't glue themselves together.

"Interesting."

"That's all you've got? You had tea with him, he gets a call, he walks away to take it, and then manages to somehow get out of the inn with no one seeing him until I found him dead. And that's interesting to you how?" I didn't want to be confrontational with the one person who might be able to help me and had always been my sounding board and my tether to the world when I sometimes felt totally out of whack. But she was acting strange, and I didn't like it.

She shook her head and then bit on her bottom lip. "Who called him? That's what I would like to know. And why did he have to leave to take the call? He's talked to any number of people throughout the years during our annual first tea on the afternoon of the beginning of the conference. I've heard him talk to agents, fans, and his publicist, as well as his attorney one time and his nephew." She grabbed the pendant at her neck and sawed it back and forth on the chain. "Did someone call him and ask him to meet them somewhere in town, like the ferry dock, and then they killed him?"

"All worthy thoughts and questions, I'm sure," I said. "But I have no way of getting answers to any of them. Last I saw his cell phone, the police had it, and I highly doubt they'd turn it over to me so I could search through it. I'm sure they're doing just that themselves right now."

"Dead end. No pun intended." She shivered, and I knocked on the inside of the freezer door.

"We'll talk more about this later. For right now, I have to get out of here and entertain our guests with some great speech that I forgot where I put it. I'll wing it since it's not any different than any Poobah has ever given over the years."

"I'm sure it will be fine, dear. Just say a few nice things and let them dive into the open bar. They'll forget you even exist."

There was a certain truth to that, but since this was my first year running the conference and hosting it, I had wanted it to be as close to perfect as possible so Poobah would know he had done the right thing by entrusting the inn to me. I had a feeling I was not exactly up to snuff at the moment. Perhaps that was a bad choice of word, but I wasn't changing it.

No one had come to open the door yet, and Aunt Hellen had started to shiver in earnest. I banged on the door this time instead of just knocking. Two seconds later, which felt more like an eternity, Glennis opened the door.

"I was wondering if you all had decided to just ride out the storm in there, maybe hibernate like a bear." She laughed, and I tried to, but my teeth were chattering too much.

I scooted past Glennis, not waiting for my aunt to follow. Wedging the oven door open a crack, I stuck my hands over the vent and enjoyed the heat for just a minute. Aunt Hellen hip-checked me over, and we both stood at the oven until we were at least a little bit warmer.

"Do you have any idea why someone would want Owen dead?" I asked her quietly as we stood shoulder to shoulder.

"Not really." She shook her head and sighed. "He was a nice enough person and generally liked. I'm not certain why anyone wants anyone dead in real life, so I wouldn't be the right person to ask about that kind of thing, but this is so strange. Who was he talking to, and why did he leave?"

"All things we need to know. Poobah and Uncle Vince think it's someone here." There was a gasp behind me, but I ignored it, knowing Taylor's voice well enough to no longer be nervous every time she gasped because she gasped at almost everything. She'd once screamed in outrage when the last paper towel would not easily come off the cardboard tube. It was her M.O.

"It would, of course, make sense if it was a guest, but these people have been meeting for years." I continued. "Even the younger ones have been here for at least three or four years, so who would hold a grudge for that long and feel like now was the right time to kill a fellow writer?"

"And antiquitarian." Hellen pursed her lips.

My mind jolted back to the book that Poobah had been looking for in Owen's room. Did that have something to do with his death? Where was the book if not in his room and not in my safe? Although I couldn't be completely certain that it wasn't in his room since we'd only taken a quick glance around before the police descended on us, and then Norm descended the stairs in a very clumsy way.

The dinner bell rang, interrupting my thoughts. Well, Glennis rang the dinner bell, interrupting my thoughts when she also smacked me in the arm.

"You have duties, and they aren't about figuring out a murder. Get out there and do your speech, and let the police figure out whodunnit." She sashayed back to the stove as if the conversation was over and she was the winner. We'd see about that.

Chapter 8

I entered back into the room just as everyone scattered away from the kitchen door. I'd let that go and see what kind of information I could get out of the room once I made my speech. With a room full of writers who often dealt with motivation and sleuthing, even if they were writing a children's book about fairies, they had to have some concrete ideas and maybe some places I could start looking so I wasn't running scattershot.

"Thank you, everyone, so much for being here for another wonderful year of community, learning, and networking. We at the Charmed Inn are always happy to host you and that you choose to stay with us every year. It's a highlight." I took in the room and could honestly say, normally, it was a highlight. I had looked forward to this eclectic group being here for their weekend. I could have done without the murder, though.

"Before we get this thing rolling, I also want to make sure you know you're safe here, and we will do everything we can to make this weekend the one you looked forward to."

There was a scoff from the crowd, but I couldn't tell who did it, and when I zeroed in on each face in front of me, no one looked away or looked guilty. I'd prove it to them then. I didn't like naysayers any more than anyone else did, but I also often took them as a challenge. If that scoff was supposed to be a gauntlet, then I was picking it up and waving it around aggressively.

"Please let us know if there is anything we can do to make your stay more comfortable. You have a lot to look forward to, and I hope it meets your dreams and wishes."

"Well, I won't lie, I didn't think I was going to be part of a murder investigation. A murder mystery-type weekend isn't my thing. But I'll do my best to not say anything negative about you and yours in the reviews I post once we leave." Erma. Of course, it was Erma talking. Was she also the one who had scoffed? I didn't think so, but the jury was out on that one.

"I would appreciate that," I said through gritted teeth and a very wide smile. "We'll celebrate Owen's life later this evening with tea and crumpets after dinner if that works for you."

There was a murmur of approval, thankfully.

"Ha! If we don't get dead from strangling, then I guess we could get dead over too much sugar." Erma again.

"You don't have to eat the crumpets if you don't want to, Erma. No one's making you." Paddy jumped in before I had a chance to say anything or do anything more than growl at the back of my throat. For once, I appreciated him, and that was saying a lot.

Aunt Hellen sighed next to me, and if I was thinner or even just smaller, it probably would have toppled me over. I did not understand her draw to him, but I didn't have to.

"Okay, so that's the end of my speech. How about we dig into this amazing meal Glennis put together for us and then we'll do the life celebration and then it will be free time until tomorrow when the classes start?"

That was all it took for everyone to turn from me and sit back as my kitchen brought out plates and put them in front of each person. Since Poobah was already in my chair and I needed a minute to myself without anyone over my shoulder, I motioned to Glennis not to bring out my food. I'd grab it from the kitchen. I wanted to be in the library, and there was a table there where I could eat. Alone.

I highly doubted they would have any new information to share on the murder. Even though I had wanted their ideas on where to start, I had a feeling they weren't going to stick in my chaotic brain if I didn't take a minute to myself to just come back down to normal. Plus, Poobah was in there if anyone had any good ideas. They were here all weekend. I could ask after they'd loaded themselves up with food.

I gave a little wave as I exited the dining room again and made my way to the kitchen. This time, no one moved, and I could see them all sitting around the table, eating, laughing, and talking amongst themselves. I had no way of knowing what they were talking about, but Hellen was out there, so she could tell me if anything happened that I needed to know about. I'd have to leave it there so I could take a minute and get my bearings back.

I used a tray instead of the rolling cart this time, as there wasn't that much I wanted to bring with me. Glennis had outdone herself with the rosemary chicken and her delightful mashed potatoes and sauteed asparagus. I wasn't that hungry, but I knew I'd have to eat something because I had a feeling I was going to be up late tonight looking around and trying to figure out what might have been missed in the death of Owen. And I needed to know where that book was. Oh, and also, who my sidekick was, so I could keep them close. Nothing to it.

Sitting in the fluffiest chair in the library, I glanced out the huge windows to the left. I appreciated the lowering dusk over the river. It was peaceful and would be again once we figured out what had happened to Owen and who had done it.

He was a writer but also a genealogist and an antiquitarian. There was the book that he'd been talking about forever, according to Poobah. Supposedly, it had been in his family for generations and held secrets and possibly a treasure map to a fortune that had been lost on its way down the Susquehanna years ago.

For how shallow and navigable the river was, I was surprised no one had accidentally stumbled across it. Of course, there was every possibility someone had and just hadn't told anyone of their find. I'd asked Poobah more about what he knew, and he said Owen had been on the hunt for it for as long as I'd been alive. And he had promised everyone on the online chat they had set up that he was going to show it to them when he found it. So where was it? Had he definitely found it since Poobah recognized the box it would have arrived in? And was that why Owen was dead?

So many things swirling through my head as I savored the chicken and the silence.

I just wished that when I went back to re-enter the fray, I would have come up with some answers. But no matter how many books I trailed my fingers along on the shelves, none of them sparked like they had before. They didn't even vibrate, and there was absolutely no humming. I was going to have to do this like normal people did and just dive into the who, what, where, when, and how.

Finally, I was done with my dinner and knew it was time to go back to the dining room. Suddenly, the chicken was sitting a little heavier in my stomach than it had before, but there was no helping it.

I made my way back along the hallways, taking the trail that I'd traveled enough there should be a worn path in the hard-wood floor. I heard a commotion before I made it to the last turn into the dining room and picked up my pace to see what the heck was going on.

And I came face to face with Norm again, and this time he was beyond irritated. If I knew him, and I did, no matter how much I wished I didn't, he was pissed.

Join the club, buddy.

"Norm, what can I do for you?" I broke into his pacing and put myself where he would not be able to walk by me without pushing me out of the way.

"I need to look at the inventory your dealer guy brought, and he won't let me. Said I need a search warrant, and even then, I can't touch any of his books."

My gaze wandered around the room looking for Demetri Petrovski. When I found him, he simply shrugged and raised his hands like this was none of his fault.

"Is there a truth behind that statement?" I asked Norm. "Do you need a warrant or something to have access to things that don't belong to you?"

"Well -"

"Yes or no?" And I had a feeling I knew which answer he was going to give me before he did. Or I wouldn't have asked the question.

He blew out a breath. "All right, yes, yes, I do need to get a warrant, or he could just let me look at his things and pass them over as being irrelevant, and I could use my time to actually find the killer instead of diddling around here."

Diddling around? Seriously, who said stuff like that? Had he been watching too much Barney Fife?

"I'm not sure what to tell you then. Demetri has very expensive things in his possession. And if you're going to take anything because you think it's significant to your case then I would think you'd want to do this from the beginning the right way." I expected the nasty look he shot at me since I rarely got anything else. I did not, however, expect him to nod at me and then leave.

"I'll be back with it," Norm said as he walked to the foyer. He turned with his hand on the doorknob. "You'd better have everything in those cases exactly like I saw them tonight, too. No taking anything out or hiding anything you don't want us to see. Got it?"

The dealer nodded shortly but didn't say anything. Honestly, with that kind of attitude, I'd take everything back out to my car and drive it out into a field where no one would ever be able to find it again. How rude.

But Demetri held up his hand as soon as I turned to him. "Do not worry about it. I have dealt with police before, and he is certainly not the worst specimen, though he is riding a line there that he might not want to cross. I have nothing to hide, but because of my insurance, I have to have the proper paperwork before anyone can handle my wares, or they are not covered if something were to happen to them out of my sight."

"As long as you're sure?"

"I am positive that this is the way to go. I don't know that he'll be able to get a warrant, but I'm sure it will benefit his experience in these kinds of things to try."

Honestly, I'd rather Norm never have to use these skills again, but this time, at least, I needed him on the top of his game, which he wasn't as far as I could tell, and that was saying something since my primary exposure to this kind of thing was through books and screen time.

If nothing else, it resolidified my need to know what happened and who made it happen. There was something here, and it needed to be found out. I wasn't saying I was the one to do it or that I'd even know what to do with the information if I actually got it. But if Norm was going to harass my guests and blame my friend and possibly me for the death, then there was nothing else I could do but dive in.

Crap.

I stood outside the dining room, and it sounded like people were still talking and eating, so they didn't need me at the moment to start the celebration of life. I could take a minute and see if I could talk Glennis into making me a cup of hot chocolate. I considered tea, but since that was the last thing Owen drank today, I was going to give it a little time before I dove into that beverage again.

"I think we should tell her," I heard through the kitchen door as I put my hand on the panel and started to push. I held myself back for a moment to see if they might say anything else. It sounded like Clara, and she didn't always talk to me, but she often talked to Glennis. To the point that sometimes Glennis asked if she could get her a muzzle. I, of course, turned that request down. Although I could understand wanting one because I had the same desire when Aunt Hellen went on a tangent, and I would be the first to muzzle Paddy if given a chance.

"I understand, but she has a lot going on. Tomorrow would be soon enough, and maybe we should look into the possibility before we say anything. No need to send her off on a wild goose chase when she has so many other things going on."

I pushed because there would be no better time than now to jump right on in and demand that they tell me.

"What is it that I need to know? At this point, I'd rather have it all up front instead of being hit with anything new tomorrow."

Glennis groaned, and Clara went coy. That was never a good sign.

"Well, it seems that there was some kind of tryst going on earlier. We heard it through the dumbwaiter, and it sounded like someone was cooing to someone else. We thought you should know."

"We thought nothing of the kind," Glennis said and shook her head. "The first rule in owning an inn is that nothing is your business unless it becomes an issue, Clara. Until you learn that, you won't learn much else around here."

Glennis always had solid advice, but not always in a constructive way.

"I think we're going to have to throw that rule out this time around, Glennis. I need to know anything and everything you hear and see. We have to figure out what happened to Owen and who did it, or it might happen again."

She slapped a hand to her chest. "You don't think it's a serial killer, do you? You told Vince he was not right in the head for considering that earlier."

I hadn't wanted to believe it, but if it got her moving, then I wasn't above using it to my advantage. "I don't know, but I also don't want to find out who's next *after* they're dead. So, let's share the info you have, and I'll try to make sense of it and share it with the police department." I didn't promise when I'd share it, so I felt safe in the way I'd phrased that.

"The only reason we heard anything was because the dumbwaiter doesn't seem to be working correctly." Glennis crossed her arms over her chest and stared at me. Was this somehow profound? Was I supposed to be overwhelmed with guilt and panic that the one thing in the hotel that rarely got used all of a sudden couldn't be used at all? Huh.

"I'll go look at it. What's the big deal with telling me?"

Glennis harrumphed. "You don't need any other things going wrong around here, and since we don't hardly ever use it, I thought it could wait until after everyone was gone home."

I was a little baffled by her issue with telling me, but Glennis could get like that sometimes.

"Okay, well, I'm glad I know, and I'll look into it. Anything else I need to know?"

"Nope." Glennis shot a look at both Clara and Taylor. "Nothing else."

"You'd tell me if there was?" I asked.

"Eventually," Glennis said and then smirked.

"I'm totally serious. I need to know about things. I want this to go fabulously too, but if underneath it's toxic, then that might help me in the moment but not in the long run."

Now she hummed and looked at the ceiling like I'd said something profound, which I hadn't.

"Point taken. Yes, we will tell you anything we hear during the weekend, and any issues that come up, you can handle. I'm not sure it was a tryst we heard, just people talking to each other in lowered voices, but that could be anyone. Clara was the one who came up with the embellished story. If we hear anything more or hear it again, we'll let you know."

Thank goodness my employee was going to let me run my inn the way I wanted to.

However, that wasn't totally fair since Glennis had been here for a long time, and while I'd worked here on and off, I had not had nor did I have her vast experience, and I could barely make a grilled cheese much less the amazing food she made on the daily.

"Thank you, Glennis. And thanks to both of you, also. I know this weekend is one of our biggest. And also that it can be the hardest, so I appreciate anything you do, and I swear next week will feel like a vacation compared to this." Or at least I hoped so. Maybe I shouldn't have promised anything.

I left them to their own devices and went in search of the issue with the dumbwaiter. I'd checked in on the party from the television in the kitchen. Everyone seemed to be lingering over dinner and drinks, so I had a little time to check on the dumbwaiter before I was needed anywhere else. Maybe I could even go to the police station tonight and avoid seeing Norm. And if there was an issue with the dumbwaiter that was a quick fix, I could ask Dean to help me with it in his maintenance brilliance.

This thing did come in handy if someone was looking for breakfast in bed or a celebration. But we didn't use it that often because I preferred people to eat downstairs in the dining room instead of in their rooms. Less mess and less chance of something getting missed in the cleanup. Plus, my rugs in each room loved me for not having full-on room service. So did my kitchen staff. Heck, so did I.

The device was in the wall and traveled from the kitchen to the second floor at the top of the stairs. It could also go to the third floor, but people rarely stayed there. It enabled our staff to be able to not hoof it up the stairs with their hands full of dishes and heavy platters or even a fragile tea set up. The platform had blocks on it so that you could wedge the food or drink in there and then push a button in the kitchen to have it smoothly move up to the next floor. It was slow, but that wasn't a bad thing when you had a tray with tea and milk and sugar and sticky buns with cream that needed to not get rocked on its way up.

Using my fingers, I pressed lightly on the panel to open it like a garage door. It didn't budge. Perhaps that was part of the problem. I probably should have asked Glennis for more info before I just came up and tried to handle this. I wasn't going back downstairs at this point, though, so I jiggled the knob on the dumbwaiter door. There was a quiet cracking noise, and I hoped I hadn't just broken it. That was overshadowed by the fact that the door sprang up, and under one of the blocks was a yellowing page covered in scrawling spidery writing. It looked like a journal entry from many years ago, and when I touched it, the sparkle could have lit an entire town. The words that rose above the paper, though, almost stopped my heart: *Be very careful. There is a wolf in the house that's ready to snap.*

Well, color me red.

Chapter 9

To say that I was not used to the messages coming to me from books like this would have been an incredible understatement. Normally, I would read a sentence like "He crushed her to him and sealed her lips with his kiss," and from that, I'd have to answer the question of whether today is a good day to wax my car. I would mull the letters over, and the message would eventually come to me that, yes, today is a good day for waxing as I hoped the woman in the scene had also waxed her upper lip if she needed that, and hopefully, she'd considered waxing her legs just in case of this very thing happening. So, it was a bit of guessing, a bit of deciphering, and a bit of never answering tough questions or issues just in case I interpreted something wrong.

I had never, in all my years of reading, searching, and intuiting, had the words literally rise off the page and glow like a handful of lightning bugs trying to guide me through the darkness.

And I couldn't say I loved the messages they were bringing since both so far seemed to mean trouble for me and a need to be far more careful than my normal carefree. I was about to ask what the hell was going on when I stopped myself because I did not want to tempt the universe to try and answer that one just yet. I was still trying to digest the wolf aspect and attempting in earnest to also not run screaming from the house and never again touch a thing with letters on it. Never.

I sat down on the top step of the staircase and held the paper in my hand, staring at it as I made every effort to process what it was saying. There was a wolf in the house. Okay, so the murderer was someone who was here and someone who would have had access to not only Owen but would have known where he was and what he was doing when they called his cellphone and got him to leave.

But that snap part was holding me in check. Snap, as in mentally? Or snap, like using the jaw to take a chunk out of something? Because both could be valid, I had a distinct feeling that I needed to know which one I was dealing with so I could be ready to take on whatever we were in for here at the inn.

The letters continued glowing like sprinkles of Tinkerbell's fairy dust, and I was fascinated by them. I should have been more concerned about the message, and really, I was. But I couldn't help poking at the letters and having them burst apart and then move back together to form the word when I moved my finger out of the way. How did this work? Was it a spirit sending the message? The universe? I thought it was always just my ability to interpret since that was essentially what a bibliomancer was, but this was different. This was bigger than grabbing a phrase like "She walked out the door" and knowing that meant the person who wanted to choose between bacon and sausage might want to consider the links instead of the bacon. Link equaled walking along the links of a golf course, which then went to sausage instead of bacon, which might have been the choice if the phrase on the page had been "It was crisp outside and filled with a fragrance she couldn't forget."

See what I mean? Not easy. But doable. This however was not easy or maybe even doable because it didn't ring in my head as an answer, only as a warning, and I was not a fan of those. Then again, I wasn't a fan of being in situations where I needed a warning either, so there was that, too.

I rested my head against the wall and watched the letters fade back into the page of spidery script I now held on my lap. What to do? What to do? It wasn't like I could go to Norm, who I didn't want to go to under any circumstance. But I couldn't go to him now and say, oh hey, so this page fell out of the dumbwaiter, and it talked to me, and I think it's someone in the house that was being a wolf, so if you could look into that, it'd be great k thx bye.

Ugh.

And yet, Aunt Hellen was being flaky, and I really didn't want to involve Poobah more than he already was. Who was that freaking sidekick?

They could show up any time now!

I thumped my head against the wall just a tiny bit and thought of the people in my life who might fit the bill. I had aunts and uncles and grandparents and staff. None of them would work with me in a way that I thought would be productive. If my oldest sister were here or even the younger one, I could see roping them into helping but, each was off living their own lives, and I was not going to ask them to come in on the fly just because of floating letters.

I shut my eyes and tipped my head back far enough to make me feel like it might roll off at any second.

"Roxy?"

I heard my name called from the bottom of the stairs, and it hit me. Dean. Dean was the sidekick. He had to be. And there he was, standing at the bottom of the stairs even though he should have been home resting for tomorrow when he'd have to go back to work.

Surreptitiously, I shoved the page under my butt and hoped that, for one, he hadn't seen it and, for two, I had not damaged it. I might think he was my sidekick, but I didn't know if Sherlock shared every thought with Watson. Sometimes, you have to keep some things to yourself.

"Dean, what are you doing here?" That might not have been the nicest thing to say or the best way to ask but the words tumbled out and I couldn't take them back.

Fortunately, he laughed and ducked his head, grabbing the back of his neck, which gave me enough time to remove the page from beneath me, fold it quickly, and then shove it into the front of my shirt, actually into my bra, but that was between me and my undergarments, no one else needed to know.

"Actually, I was going to ask you the same thing."

"Um, I'm here because this is my inn, and I have guests?" Where else did he think I was supposed to be?

"No, I mean on the steps when you have all the guests? Your aunt answered the door when I knocked and said everyone was asking when they're going to have the celebration of life. I was sent to find you."

Now was the wrong time to groan, but I did it anyway.

"Hey, if you need a minute or something, I can tell Hellen to hold them off with more drinks. I'm sure they can wait a little longer." His forehead crinkled in concern, and I was reminded again that he was one of the nicest people I had ever met. Always looking out for others, always anticipating what people might need, and handing it to them before they could even ask.

I would not be against having someone like that as my sidekick.

"I'm hiding." I said quietly, and he came up the staircase a few steps.

"Hiding? Why?" He took a few more of the steps two at a time and then sat three steps below me, facing up. In the subtle hall light of the open staircase, his look of concern hit something in my chest and lower places. I nearly scoffed at myself. Needing a sidekick was one thing, and that would be the only thing. I did not need any kind of partner, and he was off-limits as far as I was concerned.

"I needed a minute, and then Glennis told me the dumb-waiter was broken, so I came up to see …" I trailed off because he had already mounted the rest of the steps, sidling by me and aiming right for the dumbwaiter. Of course, he had. I should have figured that out before I opened my mouth.

I also should have looked at the unit more in case there was another page.

I rose and peeked over Dean's shoulder without crowding him. Or at least I thought I had not crowded him until he turned around, and I was face to chest with his very firm, broad chest. I made fun of his last name about being a Chester of men since that was how last names had been constructed long ago, but it had always been a joke. Until now.

Hoo boy. That was an impressive chest. Not too wide, not too hard, but just right. It occurred to me that I had only hugged Dean once, and that was when Poobah had been sent to the hospital. I'd fallen into his arms because I had needed a sanctuary to be scared in. My family often looked to me as their rock. I was the white sheep in an entirely black sheep family. Everyone else had many interests and traveled all over the world. They did things on a whim and let the chips fall where they might. Me? I was the one who was always at home, ready with a hot cup of tea or a cookie or even a fully cooked meal courtesy of Glennis's wizardry in the kitchen. I was a place to come to fall apart or work on putting yourself back together if needed. But I rarely needed that myself, as I was as constant as a straight line into eternity.

But Dean had held me that day as I sobbed, and I don't think I had ever truly thanked him for that.

Now, of course, was not the time, and it was also not the time to think I could sneak another hug, this one entirely for me and not because of grief but because of desire.

Whoa, now, down girl.

I shook my head at myself and my ridiculousness.

"What's a no?" Dean asked, not taking a step back but looking down on me. He was over six feet tall, and I barely topped five feet (five feet and one-quarter inch, thank you very much). Part of me wanted to bridge that gap between us, and part of me wanted to step away. Except I couldn't remember how close to the stairs I was and did not want to take a tumble down like Norm had earlier.

I cleared my throat. "Um, nothing is a no. I was just shaking my hair out while I thought about what might be wrong with the dumbwaiter." Not impressive, not good on the fly here.

"Okay, well, did you want me to work on the dumbwaiter?"

"Oh, I hate to do that to you when you're off hours right now. We won't need it, so let's let it rest until after the weekend." That last part came out more as a question than a statement, but I was fine leaving it there because everything seemed to be a question lately.

"I'll put it on the schedule for next week then. You're sure you don't want me to fix it now?"

"You don't have any of your tools, and I have a full house. If it's going to need hammering or something or tearing it out of the wall to see what's going on, then I'd rather not do it while everyone is here. It's one thing to fix a necessity like the water heater or something, but this can wait."

Finally, he was the one who stepped away from the dumb-waiter, and I felt myself slowly releasing the breath I'd been holding. Well, the breath I held after I inhaled and got a whiff of the very essence of what Dean was.

And if that wasn't an unsettling thought, then I did not know what was. This was my best friend, the guy who ate dinner with me sometimes and put together puzzles when we didn't have anything else to do. The guy I'd told myself was better as a friend than as an unrequited crush. We didn't talk much about dating and that kind of thing. I hadn't dated in years, and whatever he did was up to him, so I only listened if he wanted to talk, but I didn't ask.

All of that was irrelevant, though, because it would never happen. I'd just come into owning the inn, and I had way too many things to do and be and see to put any time into a rela-tionship. Which also made this a moot point because to be in a relationship, you had to have two people who were interested in each other that way, and I knew without a shadow of a doubt that Dean had never tried to make a move on me. And when we'd hugged, it had felt like a brother or a sibling in general, not a hot and flashy moment to build on.

I was exhausting myself and had no one to tell since normally I would tell Dean, and this time, I couldn't.

Where was I? Oh, right, get him away from the dumbwaiter.

"Well, thanks for coming over. And thanks for finding me, and thanks for offering to fix the thing, and thanks for waiting to do it until later. Oh, and thanks for not being angry that I let you in the library and never came back." I had a sinking feeling I sounded as ridiculous as I feared.

Then Dean shrugged those lovely shoulders. "No big. You know I'm always happy to help in any way I can, especially if it's a repair thing. I haven't met a dumbwaiter yet that I couldn't wrangle into shape. And the sandwiches were just the right thing since I hadn't had lunch."

He chuckled, and I chuckled with him even as I was trying to figure out if his wrangling could extend to other things. Oh my word, I needed to get out of here now!

"Well, I'd better go down and do that celebration of life thing."

"I'll come with you, like a sidekick. If anyone messes with you, I'll be there like Robin to your Batman."

I stared at him. Was that a clue from the Universe? Was Dean the one the book had been referencing when it said I had a sidekick I needed to keep close? As much as I was the white sheep in a black sheep family, Dean had jokingly called himself the same, though I didn't know what his family's black sheepness entailed. In fact, now that I thought about it, he stayed away from most conversations that involved anything before he'd moved here.

I'd have to think about that, but not right now. That could wait until after the celebration was done, and I headed to my room for the night until someone needed me for something.

That was one of the things I did not love about running the inn, but it was small potatoes compared to how much I loved the rest of the job. And this weekend was usually pretty low-key with midnight needs. Hopefully, it stayed that way since I really needed to rest and figure some things out before I went forward.

"I appreciate any help, of course."

He smiled, and it hit a little different, and I was not prepared for that. Now was most certainly not the time for my stupid and dormant, I might add, libido to wake up from hibernation. I was not going there. The end. Period.

Back on track.

"I will keep you in the loop, sidekick, and we'll do some Batcave work. Or would you rather be the Thelma to my Louise?"

It was an old movie reference, but it fit the situation potentially. It also distracted me and my errant body from paying too much attention to the way his gray eyes sparkled when he crinkled them with his smile.

"Celebration of life!" I nearly yelled it like a toddler yelling a word they had just learned.

"Yep, that's where you were heading." He peered at me with his hands on those hips and then cocked his head. "Are you okay? We don't have to look into anything involving the murder if you're uncomfortable. Or I can do some looking and just report back if you'd prefer."

"No, no, no, that's okay. I'm good." I pulled at the collar of my sweater. "Just trying to get my thoughts together for the celebration. I'm good. Thanks!"

He dropped a hand on my shoulder. "You're always good. I depend on that more than I can tell you."

I had to get away before I did something stupid, so I stepped out around him and started down the stairs, hoping he'd follow. I did not want him looking at the dumbwaiter further until I had a chance to make sure nothing else had been left in there. And I needed him downstairs so I could usher him out of the house before I did something I couldn't take back.

"Well, thanks for coming by." I held the front door for him, and he gave me that cocked-head, slanty-eye look again.

"You're sure you're okay? You seem a little off."

"Positive, I'm fine. Just have a full brain, and it's been a long and busy day. I'm sure it will all look different tomorrow."

"Okay, I'll stop by tomorrow just in case you find anything or need help looking around. I don't work until ten, so I can come by beforehand if that works."

It wasn't like I could really say no, and if the Universe was certain he was supposed to be my sidekick, then I needed to make peace with that. And I would, just as soon as I went back to not thinking of him as anything but a best friend. I added it to my list of things to contemplate this evening after everything else was gone. Right after, I made a suspect list, tried to find any info on Owen, and went through his room again. Oh, and after I checked to make sure there were no other loose leaves of a diary that people had been looking for during the last one hundred years. I had this. Truly.

Chapter 10

The remembrance went off without a hitch once I got started. Owen had been a multi-published author who shared tips and tricks and always had time to mentor new writers. He'd made a significant splash in the eighties by writing some of the Nancy Drew books as a ghostwriter. And then, he had done some of his crime fiction, becoming a bestselling author before he'd been married. He'd taken a hiatus while he'd nursed his cancer-stricken wife until she'd passed ten years ago and then found a much different landscape in the publishing world when he came back. But he'd been okay with that and had just stuck to what he loved writing. And knowing royalties didn't have to pay the bills, he could write whatever he wanted. He'd been writing a very different book over the last three years and had planned to finish it once he'd come here.

I realized as I stood in front of the crowd that I didn't know a ton more about Owen personally, even though he'd been a guest for years. So, I let others talk about him and his work. It had been short and sweet. Everyone seemed to have liked him, even if he had been a little cagey with information over the years and had hidden things until he was good and ready to reveal them in his own time. I'd tried to get ahold of his nephew, who served as his assistant earlier, but he had not answered my calls or texts. I had no idea if anyone had even let him know that Owen had passed. In fact, when I'd asked Poobah who his next of kin was, he'd had no more information than I did. After all that was done, I headed out to the interrogation, or what I thought was going to be an interrogation.

I was a little later than I had wanted to be at the police station, and when I showed up, Norm was no longer in the precinct. I'd been allowed to go home and told he would talk with me tomorrow. Good enough for me. He might have had information on Owen's next of kin, but I wasn't calling Norm to ask.

So now I was ensconced in my room. I had set myself up in the middle of my queen-sized bed with the comforter I'd bought online on my first night as the new owner of this fine establishment. It had a quarter moon hanging in a dark sky surrounded by a thousand twinkling stars. Sleeping under it made me happy, and the snuggle factor was high with this one. Moose liked it, too, so it stayed. He was currently curled up in the crescent of the moon, and I hoped he stayed that way so he wouldn't disturb the paperwork and books I'd set out around me.

Since this was the one area that belonged only to me, I'd also put candles in the window and hung drapes that were a patchwork quilt of colors ranging from pink to the deepest purple before going black. Very few people ever came into this portion of my rooms. I also had a sitting room in the front that was much more conventional, but this space was all me with lots of pillows, books, and prints hanging on the wall that reflected my favorite things like waterfalls and patterns of leaves floating on the surface of the river. Water and I had always had a wonderful relationship, and it was the element that most called to me.

I took the page I'd found in the dumbwaiter and placed it right in front of me, where I sat cross-legged in the middle of the bed with about seven pillows behind my back. If I was going to do this, I'd have to do it right. I also laid the first book that had sparkled on my right and the book on the powers my ancestors had experienced over the years to the left of that. There was something to the ritual of where things were placed and how they were placed that spoke to my need to find out everything and anything I could in this quiet time.

Moving my notebook to the left, I took my cup of brightly colored pens and placed those in a nest of a soft Afghan blanket I'd had since I was about twelve. I was ready to see if I could make the letters glow and sparkle again now that I was by myself and nothing else was going on.

I bowed my head and said a brief spell to see if I could have the door opened as wide as possible to gain information, then blew out a breath and opened my eyes. And nothing happened when I passed my hand over the text on either the page or the book. Freaking A!

I tried again and again, and nothing.

I still took the notebook and tried to remember exactly what had been said in both pieces. I was pretty sure I got the right gist down, if not the exact words. I was Sherlock and needed to keep my Watson by my side, and I had a wolf in the house that was ready to snap. I should have written them down earlier when they'd actually happened, but I'd been a little busy and a little sidetracked by the sparkly letters. That had never happened before.

So, I picked up the book of my ancestors and paged through it while I continued to will the letters to rise from the pages again. Nothing.

Running through the various sections of the few bibliomancers in my line gave me nothing either because unless they didn't write it down, it had never happened before. Leave it to me to have the weakest talent but the weirdest version of it.

I dropped back against the pillows and stared up at the ceiling. Years ago, in a different room, I'd put stars above me, the ones that glowed. I'd put them in various patterns to match the sky, or spell out words, or make pictures. I'd been a preteen, and my parents hadn't ever stopped me from rearranging my room or my environment to fit whatever I felt I needed at the time. Now, I kind of wished I had the stars above me again so they could tell me what I needed to know.

Sighing, I wondered what I was going to do next. I had no plan, and I absolutely hated having no plan. But how did you plan for these kinds of things? Even Jessica Fletcher had just kind of followed along as the clues came to her, but she always at least had a jumping-off point. I had nothing, and it was driving me crazy.

Although ...

I leaned over to my nightstand and grabbed my computer. I hadn't thought I'd need it since I was trying to do everything by hand. It made sense because that was where my talent was always most prevalent. But maybe I should think outside the box if I was going to act outside the box for the first time in my life. I was a rule follower, a rock, as my sisters called me. I always did the right thing and would always ask permission before I'd ever wait and ask for forgiveness. But maybe this time I had to look at things from a different perspective.

First and foremost, I needed to find more information on who Owen was. That speech this evening had really highlighted for me how little I knew about him and how little really anyone seemed to know about him.

Sure, he was nice and, as some had said, a little cagey, only willing to do things on his timetable, but there had to be more out there about him and his place in the larger community outside the writers' group. It did highlight for me also, though, that while I thought I knew everyone here from being around them for years, that also wasn't true. Plus, there were some newbies I had to take into account. And while I had promised to keep everyone here safe, it was feeling more like it had to be someone already in the house who had done the deed. I really didn't want to believe that, but who else could it have been?

And yet, how could I truly think Erma or Francine or any of the other people who had been spending this weekend together for decades would turn out to be a killer? And why now? Unless it really did have to do with the diary and the treasure attached to it. But the diary he had said that he was going to share with everyone did not have the map in it from what Poobah said. I was pretty sure that he would have crowed to the heavens if he'd managed to find that one.

It was so confusing, and my brain was starting to hurt. I wrote a list of everyone who was here and anyone in town I could think of who might have had a beef with Owen. It wasn't a big list in any way, shape, or form, but it at least made me feel better. Especially since I couldn't get the diary page to light up with the sparkly letters again.

As I was stacking all the materials into a pile to move them to my dresser, someone started banging on the door in the sitting room. I bobbled the pile, and as it cascaded to the floor, swirling letters rose from the pages, then sank right back down. All I managed to see was the word "care" before more banging sounded on the door.

"Coming!" I yelled. I wasn't in the main part of the inn, but a room off the conservatory. And yet, with how loud the person was being, others might wake up and come around to see what was going on. I did not want that. What on Earth could be so important that it required trying to break down my freaking door?

Throwing a robe on over my pajamas, I hustled from my bedroom into the sitting room and yanked the door open.

On the other side, standing in the hallway with her hair a chaotic mess around her face and her chest heaving, was Aunt Hellen. We stared at each other for a second, her hand still raised to brutalize my door once more if I hadn't moved fast enough. Her eyes were red and a little wild. In all my years, I had never seen her quite this disheveled. What was going on?

"Um...hello?"

The second turned into almost a minute, and I saw her work to control her breathing and pat her hair down. It didn't make a difference, but I wasn't going to be the one to tell her that.

She shoved me out of the doorway and strode into my sitting room like she owned it. Throwing a bag onto one of my needlepoint antique chairs, she thrust her hands into her hair and yanked so hard I was afraid she'd hurt herself. Thankfully, she let go after about five seconds. She looked at me and said, "We have an issue."

Okay then. "We have a lot of issues," I returned. "They seem to be piling up. What is yours?" I could have said something about the Paddy thing and her even stranger-than-normal behavior, but I didn't want to guess wrong.

"We're going to need hot chocolate for this one. Bring the Irish Cream, too."

After I peered at her for about two seconds, she waved me off and then tipped her head back and sighed long and loud.

I made sure my pile was stacked symmetrically and securely on my desk in the sitting room and office before I went to the kitchen and made my aunt a cup of hot chocolate and one for myself. I left the Irish Cream at the bar. As an afterthought, I grabbed one of the remaining crumpets to see if that might make her feel better. I threw some cheese and a few crackers on the tray and then put marshmallows on the top of the cup. Just for good measure, I grabbed a cookbook off the shelf above the stove and blew out a breath before opening it.

"What am I in for?" No glowing letters this time, but the line about layering alternating cups of cheese and then noodles and sauce for my favorite lasagna told me that there might be a long road here and that with some patience and a little stability, I should be able to weather this and come out with something that would make everyone happy. That was good enough for me.

I put back the cookbook and picked up the tray to walk it back down the hall to my rooms. I could do this. Hellen might be a force to be reckoned with, but it was also usually a very short-lived stint in the storm, and then she'd calm down and be very rational in the shadow of her meltdown. I'd just hope for that.

But when I approached my room, I could hear sobbing, and when I opened the door, I found her lying on the floor with her arm over her eyes. Maybe I should have brought the liquor.

I set the tray down on the coffee table that I'd been gifted by my grandmother when I was twenty. I placed the cups and saucers onto the coasters I liked to collect. Or rather, people liked to send me them from their travels, so I collected them because it wasn't like I could just throw them away. I had hundreds stacked in a variety of places, but the ones I used for this sit-down were a series of cherry blossom images from Japan.

And now we waited. Except instead of telling me what was wrong, she yelled incredibly loud and then pulled at the necklace at her throat. The one that'd been given by a secret admirer she thought was Paddy. Please do not let this be about that man. I couldn't take it right now.

"Pull yourself together. It's almost freaking midnight, and we have an inn full of guests. What exactly is the issue?"

She gasped, but at least it got her to stop making so much noise. Perhaps the lasagna recipe hadn't been wrong in its use of sauce.

"Crumpet?" I held out a plate from my position on the chaise lounge on the opposite side of the coffee table.

"I made a fool out of myself." She harrumphed and then frowned at me.

"They're exceptional crumpets. Glennis used a new kind of flour, and I'm convinced it made all the difference. The guests we have for this weekend can't get enough of them. Even Uncle Vince called them divine. You know how picky he is about his sweets. I was surprised there were any left when I went to the kitchen, but since there were, I thought maybe they'd help."

"Crumpets always help. Irish Cream would have been better, though." She might not have been happy that I'd left the liquor out in the bar, but she still took the plate and then sat her rear end down on the couch opposite me.

Time to talk.

"So, I'm almost afraid to ask what brought you here at almost midnight and trying to rip your hair out, but I feel like it has to be important if you did. And I know you, so I know that sending me out for hot chocolate and liquor was your way of realizing you probably should not have come here because now you regret it and think you can handle it yourself. And you should have never come to me in the first place." I dug into my mug of creamy chocolatey goodness and fished out a melting marshmallow to pop into my mouth. It was absolutely delicious, and I would savor it while I waited for her to answer. She did much better if I didn't do more than state my case and let her come up with the rest. I loved my aunt, but she had her foibles, and I wasn't unaware of them.

She hemmed, hawed, sighed, and then harrumphed. "I am not always happy that you know me so well. It can be very irritating to not be able to skirt around you whenever I want to."

I shrugged and settled back into the chaise lounge across from her. I was here for the long haul. "I do get that, and I also understand that it's hard, but we work together a lot, and despite you saying you're not on the payroll, you know I'd put you on in a heartbeat if you'd let me. You're here for the room and board, but you do so much more, and I wish you'd let me just start writing you checks. We have the money."

She waved me off and gulped her hot chocolate, then crammed one of the crumpets in her mouth. To stop herself from saying anything? I had let her get me off the subject for a moment, but that moment was not going to last, and she knew it.

I waited again and found another marshmallow that was at the perfect melting point to scoop out of my mug with a porcelain-gripped teaspoon that I'd brought just for that purpose.

"It's lovely being here, and I appreciate the room and board, and having Glennis cook all my food makes it worth it to run the front desk every once in a while or interact with guests. I have enough money. I don't need to be paid. I'd rather you spend it on getting Dean back here to do all those repairs. I know how much he enjoys working on this old inn and how much you enjoy being near him, so that's a win-win situation, I would say."

"There are repairs that need to be done, and we're full almost all the time lately, so yes, it helps to have him around." I had been naïve enough to tell her about my crush when I'd first met Dean, running into the inn like some teenager and twirling in the middle of the foyer with my hands up near my heart and humming to myself about how freaking hot he was and also adorable. She'd caught me when I thought no one was around, and then I had to explain myself, especially when Dean had walked up on the porch and waved to me through the window, and she had said, "Oh, I see now. Nice. Very nice." And then left, singing the song about K-I-S-S-I-N-G.

I set my mug on the coffee table and leaned forward. Hellen sank farther into the couch cushions and brought her mug up to her mouth as if that would be a barrier to the question that she had to know I was going to ask and then demand answers if she wasn't quick enough to enlighten me.

But before I could say anything, she put the mug on the coffee table, leaning forward until the new necklace she'd received from that secret admirer swung forward and seemed to shimmer in the candlelight from the sconces on the wall.

"I can't get the necklace off, and it's making me do things that I don't understand."

Uh-oh.

Chapter 11

I didn't know what to say, so I sat there for a second, not saying anything.

"Can you help me?" she asked. "At least try to get it off and see if it's just my clumsy hands?"

The tears in her eyes were something I so rarely saw. I plunked down my mug and rose from the chaise lounge, not very gracefully. It probably looked more like rolling out of it, but it didn't matter as long as I could get behind her and reach the clasp.

When I went to grasp the two pieces, the thing sparked and singed my fingertip. She eeped, and I jumped back, nearly stumbling into my window.

"What the hell?" I couldn't stop myself from trying again. And again, it sparked. Not the pretty sparkles I'd been chasing all day with the texts, but like an electrical arc from the necklace to her skin and mine. Uh-oh was an understatement.

"Ow." She gulped and then squeaked. "Please let me know if you're going to try again."

"Does it do that when you try taking it off?" This was not good, not good at all. What was it, and who the hell had given it to her? Secret admirer or stealthy stalker?

"No. No, it just feels like it's cemented or soldered together. I can feel the two ends but can't separate them."

I came back around to the lounge because I was not going to put her through more pain when we both knew that thing was not coming off for me.

"What did you mean that it was making you do things you normally don't do?" I had to know what we were dealing with if we had any hope of getting it to release her. Though, to be honest, I had absolutely no idea how I would do something like that, and I highly doubted I was going to get instructions by opening a book, any book.

She shook her head and picked her mug back up. "That's why I wanted the Irish Cream."

"It can't be that bad."

"You would be a bad judge of badness then. I'm up this late because, apparently, I kept Paddy in the sitting room for hours on end, just staring at him and fawning over him until he finally escaped by pretending that he had to go to the bathroom. Glennis came in from the kitchen and asked what was wrong with me. I had no idea what she was talking about, but then she ran one of the security tapes back, and you would think I was some fangirl or the ultimate sycophant. I was all over him and hanging on his every word, trying to touch him in any way possible."

"You kept your clothes on, though, right?"

She burst out laughing and blew me a kiss. "Thank you for that, and yes, I did. You're right that it could have been worse then. Absolutely." She sighed and closed her eyes. "So, I tried to see what was happening in the tapes, and I was shocked by how I was acting. It was as if when I was near him, I couldn't help myself, but when I left, or he left in this case, it was like the link was broken. I didn't try to chase him down to test it out, but as much as I think he's cute, I have never been so obsessed with him. He's always just been someone who's nice to look at and fantasize about, but I'm fully aware that as a real-life partner, he would probably be my worst nightmare."

That was good to know and made me feel much better about her behavior this morning. However, it made me feel worse about what the necklace was doing to her and more concerned about the fact that I couldn't get it off.

I needed a book or a page (although that was new) like right now. I went back to the pile I'd made from my bed and rifled through the papers I'd spilled earlier in an effort to find the one that had shown the sparkling letters spelling out "care" before I'd yanked open my door and found Aunt Hellen. Was that message about her? Had it popped because she was coming to my door, and I needed to be ready to care for her? That would be far more direct than normal. But I'd take it.

A poof of sparkle flitted through the air and then another, like tiny fireworks, as my fingertips whisked over the pages, but I couldn't figure out which one. I softly rage-screamed and then held my breath and cleared my mind. I could do this. She was in no danger of doing anything stupid because of the necklace at this very moment, so I could take my time instead of rushing and doing it wrong.

I drew in a breath and counted to five. I released that breath on another count of five. Of course, I could be totally wrong, and she had already left my room and was out doing something completely and ridiculously stupid. I tried to find the middle ground between taking my time and hauling ass, but it wasn't easy. So, I just grabbed up all the pages at the same time and made my way back to the sitting room.

She had the locket in her palm again, but instead of running it back and forth along the chain, she was tugging on it.

"You're going to hurt yourself. Stop that." I grabbed one of the arm coverings from the couch and used it to cover the necklace where it touched her skin. "Any better?"

"I don't know. At this point, I'm equally irritated and scared, and that leads to me being anxious and wanting to do stupid things, so really, it could just be my temperament at this point."

"Did you have any kind of reaction around Owen?" I asked as I spread the pages out on the coffee table, hoping that because they and I were closer to Hellen, maybe they'd do the more concentrated glitter thing instead of the little fireworks. Or perhaps she'd see the sparkles like she had last time, and it could at least lead me to which page to focus on.

As soon as all seven pages were lined up next to each other, including the diary page and the list of people I'd made that might have been the murderer, the air shimmered above them like a cascade of gold dust had been winged up and burst over and over again with different words. I wasn't catching them all, but Hellen started saying them out loud, and I grabbed my paper and pen.

"A cup is needed. Turn the ten. Focus on the pour. When enthroned. Chaos. Care. No, not care, scare. Scare is needed to turn the ten and focus on the pour when you are enthroned." She shut her eyes and grabbed the locket. Her knuckles turned white with her grip, and I was afraid she might hurt herself in a different and mental way if she didn't let go.

I scribbled it all down and waited, though. Aunt Hellen was not a newbie at this kind of thing. She'd known enough to watch her own behavior while obviously under a spell. That was not normal with a spell powerful enough to keep you from removing an object like a chastity belt, so I'd follow her lead for the moment. Unless things got out of hand, then I'd step all over her if I had to.

When she opened her eyes again, they were hard and narrowed. "I know I asked for hot chocolate, but I think this calls for tea."

I had a small station for tea in the sitting room, just in case I wanted some and didn't want to wander the halls or have to interact with anyone. I also had loose-leaf tea, which I assumed she would want as a tasseomancer. Reading tea leaves had been something she'd done for years and years. While some people called it silly to be able to see answers of the future in what they considered a random pattern of dark brown spots, she saw a world of possibilities. And if it gave us answers, I'd make her as many cups of tea as I possibly could.

"Do you think this will work? Is there a certain amount of time they have to steep?" I asked.

"No specific time, but I will need to drink it, so get that water hot, and we'll talk while it cools enough to gulp, not just sip."

"Can do." I set the electric kettle on its stand and pushed down the tab to get the water boiling. I had several different mugs in my room, but most of them had favorite characters on them from the nineties or sassy sayings. I didn't think that was probably appropriate, so I grabbed a delicate porcelain cup from a top shelf, one that had belonged to my great-grandmother, and used it. I wiped it out first.

"Have you found anything else?" she asked.

In her flowered pajamas and a purple house coat, she reminded me so much of all the nights we'd sat and talked throughout my life. She'd always been a constant in my world, and I hated that this was happening. Murder was horrible, of course, but messing with those who were alive wasn't much better, especially with magic. But who could it be? Most of the people I knew who could do magic were related to us. I really hoped it wasn't going to be a cousin or an uncle.

"I found a page with scrawled writing on it that might belong to the diary Poobah said Owen had brought with him to show everyone."

I had forgotten that I hadn't had a chance to talk with her too much because she'd been dreamily looking at Paddy for most of the day except when we had been in the freezer together. Her intense stare told me I'd better explain myself. I told her about finding the page and the way it had told me about the snapping wolf. I also told her about the sidekick thing.

"As much as I would wish I was the sidekick, I think Dean is far more up to speed. There's something about him I've never been able to put my finger on, but I like him. He's trustworthy, and he won't steer you wrong."

"I hope you're right." I poured the water from the kettle over the leaves I'd put directly in the bottom of the cup as Aunt Hellen had taught me years ago. It wasn't like I could read them myself, though she'd tried to teach me that too, when we'd still been waiting to find out what exactly my talent was.

I also told her about the trip to Owen's room and Norm's mess-ups while I waited for the steam to subside above the cup. We looked over the pages again to see if there were any other words to write on my notepad but came up with nothing.

Finally, the tea was at the right temperature. Aunt Hellen had not been kidding when she said she was going to gulp it down. I used a screen to keep the leaves from choking her and then not being present in the cup. There was no point in reading tea leaves if they were all in her stomach.

I sat next to her as she hummed over the nearly empty cup. I could see nothing in there except clumps of brown, but fortunately, I wasn't the one doing the work here.

She swished the last dregs of tea around and kept humming, not a tune, but more of a constant rhythm. "Anything?"

"Shh."

"Right, sorry."

She used her free hand to pat my leg and then cupped the porcelain in both her hands and brought it to chest level, dipping her head to say something quietly over the cup. It was kind of like a blessing, a little offering too and a request for help. It was in a different language, and I'd never really understood the words, but as long as it got her what she wanted, I didn't need to.

"Ah." She used a spoon to swish the tea one more time and then placed the cup on the coffee table.

I waited patiently, or as patiently as possible, even thought I was about to jump out of my skin. Come on! But I didn't ask again since I didn't want her to shush me again if she was in the thinking mode of divination.

I waited another thirty seconds. I watched them tick away on the clock on the end table that had been in our family for two hundred years. This was taking way longer than I had hoped, yet I still kept myself in check. She'd tell me when she was ready, but this was killing me, just in case anyone was wondering.

Finally, she put her hands together, thanked the cup, and then looked at me. "We're going to need Vince. We can wait until tomorrow, but he's the only one who can unspell the necklace without taking it off."

"Wait, what? We need to get it off you. It can't be good to be put into a trance-like state and made to do things that you don't want to do, and even if he unspelled it, that doesn't mean the caster can't respell it if he or she is here."

She patted my leg again, and I wanted to grab her hand.

"Whoever did this went to a lot of trouble to make sure it wasn't coming off. Had the recipient been anyone else, they might have been able to do far more than they have with me. It was just circumstance and a life of dealing with people's dark side that led me to think there might be an issue. And the leaves are telling me this has something to do with the issues we're having. If I show up without it on, whoever did this is going to be suspicious of why, and then we won't be able to find out who the murderer is. I don't know if Vince can take the spell away altogether, but I at least need him to lessen it to the point where I can manage to look like I'm fawning over Paddy without actually fawning over Paddy. It will allow whoever this is to think they still have power, and maybe they'll do something they think no one will notice, but I'll be watching."

"I'm not saying it doesn't make sense. I'm saying I don't like it, and don't you dare correct me on that double negative. It was warranted."

Placing her hand on my cheek, she looked into my eyes like she had on any number of occasions when she really wanted me to pay attention. There was a certain magic in that gesture and stare alone.

"I understand, but I also know I have power of my own, and now that I know what we're dealing with, I'll be able to counter things as long as Vince can help. I hope he'll help anyway."

I scoffed. "Of course he'll help. There's no way he'd turn his back on you."

"Well, I haven't always been very helpful to him, so it would be within his right to tell me no."

"You have got to be kidding me. No way. Why would you even say that?" I knew this was starting to ride into the territory that my mother had told me I might not want to know before she and Dad left on their trip, but if there was something big here that I needed to be on the watch for (on top of every other freaking thing) then I felt I'd rather have it on the table then do the wrong thing at the wrong time because I was going in blind.

"That's not my story alone to tell you, and some things are better left in the past. Let's just say I will be very humbled if Vince helps without demanding a price." She turned her hands over in her lap and put one on top of the other. Closing her eyes, she whispered something and then fluttered her hands in the air. It was a way to end a session or release whatever she had called at the beginning to help her.

I gripped her hand. "You're going to be okay, right?" I didn't think I could take any answer, but yes.

"Yes, I will be fine. I might be old, but I'm not without my powers. We'll get in touch with Vince in the morning. For now, I'm assured I am protected from anything for the next twelve hours."

"As long as you're sure."

"Absolutely."

"How about if you stay in here? I'll give you my bed, and I'll sleep in the sitting room, so you'd have to go past me to get out of the room. What if this person calls you or something, and you can't fight it? It could be broadcast from anywhere, and if you're alone, then you could do something you didn't intend to do."

She kissed my cheek and rose from the couch. "I know you're worried, and I get it, but I promise I'm going to be okay, and the goddess is protecting me. I have faith in that. Plus, now that I know at least to some extent what it is, it takes the blinders off and will make me question everything I do. I don't want you to have to deal with me pacing or trying to talk myself through stuff if something starts to happen. I'm just right down the hall, and I promise I will be fine. Get some sleep. Use the water to make another cup of tea with the sleeping aid I made you if you need to, but rest up because tomorrow promises to be a bit more than today, and today was a lot."

I was not happy when she left the room, but I also knew I couldn't do much to make her stay. I had to trust that she knew what she was doing. However, I knew I was not going to be able to go to sleep that easily and without some distraction. I wanted to check on Owen's room too, now that everyone was asleep, and no one would be lurking over my shoulder like Poobah or trying to catch me doing anything I shouldn't be like Norm. And while I wouldn't have minded Dean along for the ride, in an effort to get a better handle on things by being able to talk it out with him, I felt like I could at least get a start. Hopefully, the wolf, whoever that was, rested right now like the other people in the house, and I could just take a little peek in the room.

What could go wrong?

Chapter 12

Creeping along my own hallways felt very strange to me, but I did it anyway, even when I told myself to knock it off. I had every right to be walking through the halls. I owned the place. I ran the place. And I could be on an errand or making sure that everyone was in for the night. I wouldn't really need to tell anyone what I was doing even if I was caught. And yet, I had always been the permission-not-forgiveness type of person. And so I was ready with an explanation in case I came across anyone because I didn't want to get caught off guard. I didn't work well that way.

I took the back stairs again to avoid the third creaky stair on the main staircase. I'd been meaning to ask Dean to take care of that and made a mental note to ask tomorrow when I saw him.

There were a lot of notes up there right now, but at least some of them had made it onto my paper, along with everything else that had happened. Had it really only been eighteen hours since I'd eaten those two donuts this morning? It felt like eighteen days.

Keeping to the center of the staircase, I reached the landing finally. I pushed open the panel that entered onto the second floor. Most of the guests were kept on this floor because it was easier to get any towels and supplies and to clean. The third floor wasn't that far above, but dragging a vacuum cleaner up the stairs or a bunch of room supplies was something I was working on not having to deal with. Dean and I had talked about putting some closets in on the third floor, and I had money in the budget for another vacuum. Plus, we had a laundry chute where the ladies dropped the sheets and towels down from any floor.

The panel appeared as a painting on the other side, floor to ceiling. It was stunning, a depiction of the Susquehanna that rose and fell right out the window and down the hill from us. There was a train in the background and a patch of islands off the shore. My understanding was that the same great-aunt who had painted the numbers on the doors had also done this painting. I didn't know much about her, but I'd been trying to make all those words work for me by putting together a history of the place and this lovely town. I hadn't yet figured out how I wanted to write it or how much I could write since some of it would be forbidden, but I was working on it, which counted as far as I was concerned.

No more distracting myself. I poked my head out of the side of the panel to make sure the coast was clear. The lights in the hallway had been turned down low so that no one would be in total darkness if they needed to leave their rooms but also not blinded if they went from the dark to the full-on lights. It was one thing I had always hated about hotels, so I made sure to put the dimmers on the lights as soon as the hotel had been signed over to me.

Walking along the hallway, I tried to keep my steps quiet. Of course, Owen's room was the farthest away, but that's just how the place was set up.

Opening his door a crack, I tried to make sure there would be no creaking and also just make sure Erma had not been right and that Owen was floating around in here. Not that I'd be able to see him since that wasn't my particular talent.

Closing the door behind me quietly, I used the flashlight on my phone to light the interior. I didn't want to call attention to myself in the room from anyone outside by flipping the lights on.

I kept the light shining on the floor and made a mental note to make sure the vacuum got run in here. There was a dusting of what I assumed was debris from the police. Either they were dusting things, or they'd just brought in a bunch of dust with them from the outside. Maybe I'd ask Micah about that if I saw him again.

Most things were neatly piled on the long sideboard cabinet I'd put in the room when I'd rearranged the furniture a month ago. He had folders and papers galore but no books. I poked around in the piles, using just the side of my fisted hand to move things around so I could see underneath without getting finger-prints on any of them. Although I had a feeling that wouldn't matter now anyway. The cops had done their thing here, and the rest would have my fingerprints all over it.

Still, I crept around and looked, feeling weird for creeping again in my own house, but not able to get myself to stop it even when I said, "Quit it, you weirdo. No one has to know you've been here, and the walls are reinforced. Plus, you're on the second floor, and no cop sitting out on the street is going to be able to see inside the building."

I blew out a breath of exasperation with myself and then got more into looking.

I scooted things left and right and saw what I thought was a leather journal. That could be helpful if he had been writing his thoughts down. He often did from what Aunt Hellen had told me, and I'd assumed whatever journaling he did, the cops would have been interested. And yet, they'd left this.

Except when I opened it, I realized why it had probably been left. It was a bank book like Poobah had used for the inn for years, and I continued using it. It had carbon copy paper and checks as well as a ledger so that all information stayed in the same place, and you had copies of everything.

I flipped through some of the pages, and it looked like Owen had not yet moved into the twenty-first century and was still writing checks by hand for his utilities and credit card bills. There were also some carbon copies where he'd written on the memo line about advertising or the guy who delivered water. There was a huge amount given to something called Caper and then a line on the ledger with an exorbitant amount coming into Owen the very next day. That looked interesting.

Should I take it with me? The thought circled a handful of times before I put it back down. But then I picked it up again. I could always return it tomorrow, and no one would be the wiser.

Suddenly a phone rang, and it wasn't the one in my hand, but it was close by. The tone was strange and like nothing I'd heard before, not something I could place. After a second or two, though, I realized it was a Muzak version of a New Kids on the Block song. Who would do that? And also, what the heck? I'd been told that Owen's phone had been taken as evidence earlier. Did he have a second phone? A burner? How hi-tech was that? I was a little impressed.

Or at least I thought I would have been if I could have stood there for a minute or two more thinking about it instead of seeing someone trying to yank open Owen's window from the ledge that ran around the building and fumbling their phone at the same time.

After a stunned second, I scrambled back toward the bed and ended up tangled in a nest of sheets, blankets, and clothes. Throwing things left and right, I did my best to at least get to my knees. Once I got that far, I stuck my hand on the mattress to my left and got one foot flat on the floor. This was taking forever!

I did get up eventually, and it probably only took five seconds, but it felt more like five years. So, by the time I got to the window, there was no one there. At this point, I would have welcomed a cop car sitting out there, watching for anything sketchy to happen and handling it.

Because something very sketchy was going on, and I was the only one who had seen it.

I didn't care who saw what anymore. I went back to the wall next to the door and flipped the lights on. The room had been tidied, and I appreciated that. It was, however, still very full of all Owen's things. I hadn't heard from his nephew, the person I'd found out was his only living relative. I'd tried calling earlier, and I didn't know if the police had gotten a hold of him. I didn't even know if he knew his uncle was dead. I didn't want to be the one to tell him. But I'd have to call tomorrow to see if he could come pick up his stuff or if he wanted me to ship it to him. I didn't know if anything was valuable enough to spend the kind of money it would take to send back Owen's steamer trunk and his papers, journals, and clothes. But I couldn't get rid of them without asking.

And all this was keeping me from calling the cops to say that I had an attempted break-in. Whoever had been on that ledge was long gone. And they must not have known what they were getting themselves into since the windows were triple locked from the inside.

Again, I was distracting myself because I just didn't want to have to deal with Norm if he decided to come out and see what had transpired.

But it was stupid of me not to call this in and at least let them know there might be someone running around the streets who had just tried to breach Owen's room. I turned the flashlight off on my phone and dialed the number for the station. This wasn't an emergency, so it didn't require 911 like I'd called earlier today with Owen's death, but it still needed to be reported.

"I think I've talked to you more in the last eighteen hours than I did in the last eighteen months," Shirleen said when she answered the phone. I was assuming caller ID since I doubted that she knew my number by heart.

"What are you still doing there? Working a double shift?"

"With all this going on, we're short-staffed, and I am doing a split shift, not a double. I got to go home and take a nap, so I'm all chipper and ready for whatever trouble you've managed to stumble upon this time, girly."

I didn't groan out loud, but I wanted to. "I was in Owen's room..." Why? Why was I in Owen's room in the middle of the night? I hadn't thought that all the way through before I'd made the call. It didn't matter, so I just continued after a brief pause. "I was in his room, and a phone rang that didn't belong to me. I thought it might be a second phone since I was told the police had taken Owen's phone earlier, but it wasn't. Someone was out on the ledge outside his window, and they must have jumped because they're not there anymore."

"Oh! That's something to report. Thank you for calling. Is he still up there?"

I hadn't looked out the window because I'd been avoiding that too, but now I had to. Taking a couple of steps that would put me even with the glass, I peeked around the tied-back curtains as if whoever was out there wouldn't see me even if I could see them. This was ridiculous.

I pulled back the curtain completely, unlocked all three locks, and then threw up the window sash like I was auditioning for the role of Santa. I sure would have been okay with running away with a dash, but it wasn't that season.

Looking to the right, I saw nothing and no one. I looked down at the street and didn't see anyone or anything down there either. But when I looked to the left, I could just make out someone clinging to the side of my brick building, precariously balanced on the ledge that circled the second floor.

"Oh, my word, there's someone out there!" I should not have yelled that as it might wake up the house, and as soon as I said the words, the person stumbled and then lost his grip and plummeted to the porch roof below. I might be paying Dean for a whole lot more than just fixing the dumbwaiter if the person was big enough to make a hole. But they weren't. They hit, bounced, and then scrambled up and swung down over the porch roof and into the porch itself, I imagined.

"I don't know where he's going, but he just hit the porch and tucked and rolled."

"I have people on the way. I was wondering if we should wait to have it looked into tomorrow, but there's no time like the present with these kinds of things."

"Don't send -" But she had already hung up on me. "Norm," I sighed and then leaned back against the wall. I had a feeling he would be the first person to show up. At least I was wearing my good pajamas because I did not have time to change before I heard banging on the front door downstairs. And to hear it up here and with the door closed meant that probably everyone else heard it too, and they'd all wonder what was happening. Not quite what I wanted to deal with.

I wasn't going to be given a choice, though. As I walked down the hallway to the front stairs, every single door opened up except for Paddy's. Everyone had questions and exclamations and wanted to know what was going on. I wanted to know the same thing, but I had no answers. I just kept going down the hall and letting everyone know there was nothing going on and that they could go back to sleep. Of course, no one listened to me. Eventually, we were a train of people tromping down the stairs, and then they crowded around me as I opened the front door to the cops. To Norm, more specifically. And he did not appear to be happy to be here. I wasn't happy either. He could join the crowd.

Chapter 13

And what a crowd it was. Everyone who was in the hotel arrived downstairs. And yet, strangely, it felt a little like a fight scene in *West Side Story*. I had my side with everyone behind me in pajamas galore, from sweats and a t-shirt to elegant night-dresses covered in silk robes, but all very colorful. Only Erma was in a pair of jeans and a sweater, but maybe that was just her style. I was just thankful everyone had clothes on in general. I could tell stories about people who forgot they weren't dressed when they opened their room door.

And on the other side was Norm with Micah at his side, both dressed in uniform.

"Did you find anyone?" I asked.

Norm bristled like a porcupine on the defense. "I wanted to see what had happened here first before we went after anyone on the streets."

Paddy cleared his throat, and I prepared myself for a speech that was not going to go over well with Norm. When did he come down? "See here, sir, I will tell you most definitely that in that decision, you have lost the element of surprise. I'm certain the trail will have gone completely cold. You should have gone after the perp on the street. By now, he or she could be long gone, and you're none the wiser." He turned to the crowd behind me, moving himself to stand next to me but facing the opposite direction. "This is why we have to help. We must all do our duty of citizen watch and see what we can find in order to hand it to the police, who will hopefully be better at processing information than they have been in gaining said information." Placing a hand on my arm, he turned me halfway so we were now facing each other. "I think it's a grand idea for us to discuss the case at meals and to collect whatever evidence and theories we can. Great idea, Roxy. I think you are on the right track to finding Owen's killer. In the end, we'll just hand him over to the police. Hopefully, by that time, they can get their act together."

Even for Paddy, that was a strong speech, and he ended it with a flourish, whisking his robe behind him and shuffling off in his navy-blue bedroom slippers.

I knew not to look at Norm for a moment or two. I could feel the heat radiating off him as his whole being steamed with anger. Yeah, well, Paddy wasn't wrong this time. Not that I'd tell him since it would only get him more situated in his position of king of the mystery. I most certainly did not need that.

"You are not investigating anything," Norm finally said from between clenched teeth.

"I'm actually not." But that was a lie he couldn't prove, so I was fine with telling it. "I simply let the guests know if they came across anything they thought might help you find the killer, they should put it into the collection box I'm setting up. I assured them we'd hand everything over to you so you could sift through and find out what might be worth looking into." It made sense. Norm knew it made sense, which just made him seethe more. I couldn't help that, and even if I could, I probably wouldn't have tried.

"Ms. Gleason ..." he started, and I turned fully to him, waiting to see how he'd finish that. A thank you would have been nice, but I doubted that was coming my way.

In the end, after about ten seconds, he said nothing, so I turned my back on him and addressed the crowd myself. "Everyone should go back to bed. I don't think the group of you out roaming the streets looking for someone is going to help anyone. You have classes in the morning, and things to do over the next few days. If you do come across any information, you can put it in the drop box, and I'll get it to the cops. I don't think Shirlene is going to want to field a ton of calls over every little thing that might not mean anything." Let Norm stew on that. Especially since Shirlene was his cousin, and she would definitely give him an earful if she was fielding a hundred calls a day about a bird flying off in the distance. Or a gum wrapper someone found on the curb that might have DNA to help solve the murder.

"I need a statement," Norm demanded, and I faced him again.

"I don't have anything really to say. I was in the room making sure all the lights were off and seeing what kind of damage you and your people had done with all the dust you brought in and making a list. I was having a hard time sleeping after what happened today, especially because we have no answers, so I did busy work." I did not mention Aunt Hellen. I didn't see her in the crowd. It was probably for the best so she didn't do anything to Paddy we couldn't explain until we couldn't get the cursed necklace off her.

"Did you see the person trying to break in?"

"Not really. I saw the person had a black knit cap on, and their ringtone was something I couldn't place initially, but then I realized it was a nineties song done as elevator music. But other than that, they scrambled away as soon as I spotted them. They got up to the second story somehow. You might want to check into that and maybe make sure there's no damage to my roof from them tucking and rolling."

I heard a series of gasps and then a bunch of whispers. Now they all knew what had happened, and they could talk amongst themselves and then let me know what theories they came up with. I needed to go back to Owen's room to gather the ledger and a few other papers to see if they meant anything, even if the cops didn't think they did. Then I needed to go to sleep. The guests were not the only ones with a bunch of things going on tomorrow.

After the night I had, my alarm rang way too early and very irritatingly from my bedside table. I tended to not need alarms, as my body naturally knew when it was time to get up, but after the day I had yesterday, I had not been willing to take a chance. Had it really been less than twenty-four hours since I'd found Owen dead on the ferry? It seemed like far longer, and who knew what today would bring?

I put on my electric kettle and stretched, working to avoid jostling Moose, who had decided to sleep right next to my head. Setting up the teacup and the regular tea bag because I was not like my aunt and hated loose-leaf tea, I went in search of what to wear today. I could be running around, and I knew I'd be doing a lot of things, but that didn't mean I had to wear jeans and a T-shirt. Unless I wanted to, of course. This was my inn now, and no matter how many times I felt like I didn't know what I was doing, the truth was I did and dressed according to what I wanted to feel like that day. I grabbed a black pencil skirt and then an art deco silk blouse. Topping it with a long cardigan, I felt ready for the day. After I had my tea, of course.

While the magic brew that made every day feel better steeped, I took Aunt Hellen's cup into the bathroom to wash out the leaves. I never had understood how she could get anything from globs of little brown dots, but since that wasn't my talent, I didn't really need to. That was for her. The book stuff was for me. I just wish I knew more about it. I had resources, but I'd ignored them and mocked my talent for years because it wasn't like I could really do anything. And yet those sparkly letters and rising text were very, very interesting, and if I wanted them to continue to work, I might actually have to dive into how exactly I was supposed to be using what I had dubiously called a gift, but maybe it wasn't as bad or ridiculous as I had thought it was.

I saw nothing in the leaves and stuck the cup under the water in my bathroom sink to clean it out. I'd take it to the kitchen as I made my way out to the festivities today, and then I was heading out for a walk and maybe some donuts if Uncle Vince showed up.

Crap! That reminded me that I was supposed to call him this morning and ask him to come over and help with the uncursing of the necklace. I grabbed my phone out of my cardigan pocket and hit the line with his name on it. He might be at the donut shop right this moment, and I'd be able to ask him to bring the apple cinnamon donuts I'd been craving.

He picked up on the second ring.

"My love, my dove, what is going on over there? The bakery is all abuzz with an intruder, death, and maybe some kind of alien invasion, though that last one came from Donnie, so you know we can't exactly trust him."

I did not think I would laugh today with all I had on my mind, but I should have trusted Uncle Vince to bring the joy no matter what was going on. Now, I also needed him to bring the magic, but I didn't want to alarm him before he got here. However, he might need something from his house to do the work I was looking for. I had no idea how these things worked outside my own process.

I sighed. I was going to have to ask. "Can you call me back as soon as you're somewhere we can talk without being overheard?"

"This sounds serious. Is everything okay?"

"Aunt Hellen has––"

"I'll be right there." And he hung up on me. I hadn't even given him a rundown of what might be needed or what had happened.

Although, after having talked with my mom before their vacation, I should have rethought asking Vince and Hellen to be near each other. I did not know what had happened years ago, but as she was related to my mom and Vince was related to my dad, there had been some ripples but nothing catastrophic. They just seemed to stay out of each other's way, though they weren't going to be able to do that this time.

He'd better be bringing donuts, though, or I'd send him back without a second's hesitation.

I put my tea into one of my favorite traveling mugs that said, "You are Simply Magical," and then made my way out of my room and into the foyer. I checked in on Aunt Hellen and found her sitting with Paddy. The necklace was still on, and she'd had to take off the armchair cover around her neck, but I saw she'd chosen to wear a scarf today and put the necklace over it so it wasn't touching her skin. Great idea. I'd have to tell her later. She didn't look like she was leaning too far into Paddy or crowding him or simpering, so hopefully, the scarf was an effective deterrent for any more shenanigans.

I did wonder who had given it to her, though, and what exactly was the curse? If it was Paddy, had he wanted more of her attention? Or had it been cursed and was activated by the first person she cooed after? I didn't think it was for all people, or even all men for that matter. It only seemed to make a difference near Paddy. But that was also something to ponder. Was it just a boosting of something she would already do on her own, and the necklace simply amplified it? Kind of like hypnosis?

Maybe Vince could tell us more once he worked his reverse magic. Once he got here. Part of me wanted to stand out on the porch and wait for him, but the other part of me knew I had duties to attend to and not enough time to do it all.

I descended the stairs, and as soon as I got to the front door, Uncle Vince was already sailing through the double doors with smiles for everyone and a huge box of donuts in his hands.

"You're going to ruin lunch," Glennis said as she walked behind me into the dining room, where she was setting things up for the luncheon that would have a speaker. And then it would be broken down to host dinner. A lot of people used us as an actual bed and breakfast. We had a bunch of different packages. But events like these came with all the bells and whistles. It was a lot of work, and I appreciated having Glennis here to do most of it. I was the delegator, and I found myself very okay with that. Especially in these circumstances, where I had things that I needed to do and not a whole lot of extra time to do them in.

I trailed along behind Vince and watched him deposit one box of donuts into the kitchen, then he came back out to the sitting room and waved to everyone in there. I did a quick headcount, and everyone was here who was supposed to be here. Except Owen. Just the thought of him made me sad. His life was taken from him. I needed to lean more on Glennis if necessary to free up time to look into things. Plus, I needed to get with Dean. Not like actually *get* with him, but meet with him. I needed to get my brain straightened out on that before I called him, or I was going to be even more awkward than I was just on a normal basis. And I wouldn't have a cursed necklace to blame it on.

Aunt Hellen glanced up as Vince marched into the sitting room, but she didn't get up. I discreetly motioned to her, but she didn't move other than to retrain her eyes on Paddy, cup her chin in her upturned hand, and then not blink at all as Paddy just kept on talking even without any input from her. He was incredibly self-centered, as I've pointed out before, but this seemed to be a little too much for him.

"I'm sorry, Paddy. I need to borrow my aunt for a few minutes."

"No, Roxy. Paddy was just telling the most delightful story about anything at all, and I don't want to miss the rousing conclusion. Whatever you need can wait."

Paddy patted the back of her hand, and her whole body shivered. I did not like that at all. What was the purpose of spelling her, and why was it working so hard even with the precautions she'd taken?

"My dear," Paddy said, and she sighed lustily. "If Roxy is in need of you, I can certainly wait to tell the rest of the story until later. We'll get back together." He lifted her hand from the table and kissed her knuckles, then smiled mischievously, almost smirky. Maybe he had been the one who spelled the locket. He could have also had someone else do it for him. What was the purpose, though? He was getting older, and maybe he wanted someone to fawn over him because no one did anymore like they used to? He wasn't bad-looking, but it just seemed odd that you'd want someone's undivided attention when it was fake.

No matter what it was, though, it was about to be broken. I would not stop until it was completely gone and back to normal.

"Come, Hellen, I require your assistance." Vince put a hand under her elbow to get her to move. She shook him off and frowned at him. She still got up, though, so I wasn't going to fight that one.

He dropped his hand and waited for her to rise the whole way and then start walking. At the last second, she turned around and kept her eyes totally glued on Paddy as she backed up to the hallway. She blew him a kiss as we rounded the corner, and then, as soon as we were clear in the hallway, the whole thing dropped.

"You did not need to manhandle me. I was walking on my own, Vince. I'm not an idiot." She stalked past him and then made the turn to take us to my rooms. He growled under his breath, but since I was close, I could definitely hear it. Maybe I should have taken the time to find out what their issue was before I stuck them together to handle something this big. Was I in for a knockdown drag-out fight? I had no idea, but we were here, and this had to be handled, or we had to at least try to handle it. Which meant they were both going to have to lower their hackles and try to work together.

Hellen threw open my door, and I was very much convinced that she would have slammed it behind her if I hadn't been following within feet of her. As it was, she turned around with her arms crossed under her chest and a frown on her face when Vince crossed the threshold. He very quietly and gently closed the door behind him, facing it and laying a palm on it for a second while he drew in a deep breath before turning back to face us.

"Who wants to tell me what the hell is going on?" He held up a hand. "Let me restate that. Roxy, my love, if you could, please tell me what's going on since this viper probably will just spit venom at me, even though I'm clearly here to help."

Hellen scoffed but didn't move from her position of complete and utter defense.

I tucked my hair behind my ear, which I almost never did anymore, but the discomfort in this room was palpable. "We think Hellen's necklace is cursed. She turns into something she isn't, or it elevates what she is on the surface and makes it far deeper than normal. She tried to take it off last night, but it won't come undone."

"May I?" He approached Hellen and put his hands out, to feel the necklace was my guess. Her whole body went stiff, but she gave him her back. I moved to face her to see how she was doing and if removing it hurt her. She cast her gaze down to the floor and then closed her eyes as he delicately pulled the necklace from where she had nestled it in the swath of her scarf.

I'd never realized how much taller he was than Hellen. Since I'd never seen them stand next to each other, and he was often on his bike in his outrageous clothes, and she was wandering around the inn dressed to the nines and in heels, I'd never seen them this close together.

He bent over her neck, using just his fingertips to feel along the clasp.

"When I tried to unhook it last night, it had an electricity that hurt her." I wanted to let him know just in case she jerked.

"I promise to take care. I won't hurt her if I don't have to."

Hellen made a scoffing noise, and Vince stopped in his gentle pursuit of the clasp. The whole world seemed to stop, actually, and then Hellen let her shoulders sag, and Vince went back to work.

He took a pencil from my stash next to the couch and used it to pull the necklace up and away from the back of her neck. "Tell me what you've been thinking since this was put on."

"So many things," she said quietly. "It's like I can't make myself stop from going full bore with any and every emotion that comes my way. And for some reason, it seems incredibly intent on making me lust after Paddy and hang on his every word."

"Do you feel sick in your stomach about that?" He pulled the pencil toward him and leaned in to get a better look at the clasp. He blew out a breath, and she inhaled sharply.

"Are you hurt?" I asked.

"No," she sighed. "No, not physically."

They reminded me of the way my dad would lean over my mom when she was cooking in the kitchen and place a small kiss on the back of her neck. My mom would hum and then turn toward her husband of almost four decades and look up into his eyes as if she could find all the answers to all the questions there.

Hellen did not look like she was going to turn around or that she'd find anything but irritation if she looked at Vince, but his eyes glistened, and he avoided my gaze when I laid a hand on his arm.

Okay, there was a lot going on here that I obviously knew nothing about. But all of that paled in comparison to needing to get this necklace unlocked and then figure out how she could still wear it to not tip anyone off to the fact we were aware of the curse at all.

Totally easy.

"There's a lot here that I don't understand, but if you let me come around front with the back of the necklace, I think I should be able to undo what's been done without damaging the necklace." Vince waited with the necklace hoisted above Hellen's neck.

"Do you think you can fix it so it doesn't hurt her anymore? Because in all seriousness, if you can't, then I say just rip it off and let the secret admirer wonder how she managed to get out from underneath the spell. I don't know that I feel comfortable leaving it there just in case they could do something remotely."

"It's not really a curse," Vince said absently. "It's more a controlling spell. It's not meant to harm her. It's meant to keep her compliant."

"Oh, I bet you love the thought of that, don't you, Vince? I'm surprised you're even willing to remove it. Maybe you could change it to your power, and then we'd all be happy. Well, everyone except me."

Wow, that was down and dirty. I would never have expected my aunt to talk to someone like that. Was it the necklace making her response sharper than it would have been if she wasn't wearing the necklace?

Vince closed his eyes and bowed his head. He did not, however, come around to the front. He simply gripped the necklace with both hands and chanted in a language I kind of knew from reading it, but it would have taken me hours to be able to decipher what he was saying. It had something to do with reducing the flow of things, and that's about all I could tell.

As soon as he was done, something popped in the room, and Hellen's head snapped up. "Oh, wow, oh wow, I did not realize how heavy that had been around my neck. Thank…" But when she went to address Vince, he had already left, pulling the door closed behind him without a single sound.

I didn't say anything because that feeling of tension still rode the air to the point that I could almost see it.

"We will not speak of this," she said, pulling her sweater tighter around her chest and tucking her arms around her like she'd fall apart if she wasn't physically holding herself together.

"Of course, Aunt Hellen." But that didn't mean I wasn't going to call my mom and ask her what the heck happened in earlier times, that this was the way they interacted with each other. Another mystery. And this one felt almost as unsafe as trying to find a killer.

Chapter 14

Back out in the main part of the inn, I watched Hellen fawn over Paddy. Although, from my vantage point, I could tell it was faked and that she was throwing everything she had into seeming like she just could not get enough of him.

I wouldn't have been able to do that on my best day, so more power to her. When this was all over, maybe she'd stay away from him. Especially if we found out that he was the person who gave her the necklace just so he could be adored.

About twenty minutes later, everyone had dispersed to their classes, and Hellen released her breath for the first time. "We need to figure out who the supposed secret admirer is ASAP and who the killer is because I don't know if I can keep that up for any length of time without losing my mind. Was I worse than before or right on target?"

"Right on the mark, unfortunately."

"Ugh. That had to be horrendous to watch yesterday. I can't believe you didn't try to snap me out of it."

Now how on earth was I supposed to answer that? I had already told her I thought she was acting too interested, but I also hadn't said anything more because it was just this side of how she'd always acted when Paddy was around. After the emotions I'd seen on her face in my room with Vince that close to her, though, I thought now would be a bad time to tease her about her proclivities. I left it alone.

"Now that everyone is occupied and the dealer is setting his things back up for after lunch, I'm going to do some sleuthing. Dean should be here any minute. Can you send him up to Owen's room when he gets here?"

"Absolutely. I will always send Dean to wherever you are."

Why did that sound so weird for her to say? I ignored it and left to go to my room, where I picked up the scrawled diary sheet and made sure Moose was where I expected him to be. I had done some reading last night from the book of my ancestors, and it was possible the page could lead me to the rest of the book if it was here at the inn. I had no idea where to start, but Owen's room would probably be best.

I was a little scared to go in there again after what happened last night. It was the middle of the day, though, so hopefully, no one was foolish enough to try to get in through the window again. Taking the back stairs for the third time in less than twenty-four hours, I peeked my head out from behind the painting just to make sure no one was up here. I didn't like the idea of people knowing about the hidden staircase. It probably wasn't a huge secret for anyone who had played here as a child, but I didn't want to find guests using it or hiding in it, so I kept quiet as I snuck out of the painting and closed it quietly behind me.

I very deliberately did not creep into the room this time. I had every right to be here, and I really did need to see about gathering all his things and putting them in storage until someone showed up for them or I knew where to send them. I'd left a message for his nephew again this morning but still hadn't heard anything. I had no idea where he was. Technically, he had originally been signed up to be here for the weekend as his uncle's assistant but had canceled at the last minute. It left me with an open room, but since it had already been paid for and the contract stipulated that there were no returns, I still had his payment on the books. However, after the horrible tragedy of his uncle's death, I'd reimburse him if he asked.

I was so deep in my head with my thoughts that I bumped into something that shouldn't have been there. A set of hands grabbed my arms and kept me from plowing into whoever this was, and I jerked to a halt.

I didn't know who I expected to see, but it wasn't a face I didn't know. Who was this? What were they doing up here if they weren't staying here?

"Don't want you falling down the stairs," he said. His voice was deep and seemed to whisper past my face. Who was this?

"I'm nowhere near the stairs, thank you very much." I shook his hands off me and moved back a step. "Can I help you? What are you doing up here?" Was he the burglar trying a more direct route since coming in the window had failed last night?

His smile did not make me feel better, and he was about two seconds away from a swift kick to the groin and then a punt down those very stairs he was so concerned about.

He seemed to get the fact that I was extremely unhappy with his presence. Holding up his hands, he took another step back from me. He'd better not run without an explanation because that would go very bad for him.

"I'm here with Erma. She brought me along to learn and to help her out if there was anything she needed. She's been having some issues lately and thought it best if she wasn't alone, just in case anything happened while she was here. I don't know if I can help with what has happened, but I'm here if she needs anything." He smiled again, and I still didn't like it, even though it was far less smirk than the first one had been.

With his dark hair and smiling eyes, he would probably have been thought incredibly handsome, but I was not in the mood to enjoy his face and hair when I didn't know if I trusted his story.

"Erma?"

"Yes."

"Erma brought you? Are you checked in?"

He laughed, and that deep voice seemed to penetrate the very air around us. What was it with his voice that made it almost a presence of its own? I felt like I'd heard something like it before, but I couldn't place it. I wasn't going to try either since this man could be an intruder, and he was still standing in front of me. At least he hadn't tried to run.

"Are you an assistant?" I asked. Owen had put his nephew on the list and paid for his room, and he had been bringing him as his assistant. With everyone in the group getting older, it wasn't out of the realm of possibility. But looking more closely at him without appearing to stare, I didn't see much resemblance between him and Erma. It was possible he was here because she was a cougar and had brought along her boyfriend, but that seemed very far out of the realm of possibility. And how did I not know he was here, and why hadn't I seen him before?

"I can almost see the smoke streaming out of your ears." He used one long finger to tap his bottom lip. So pretentious. "Let me see if I can answer some of those burning questions in your mind. I'm her sister's son, so she's my aunt. Yes, I am in her room, but believe me, there is nothing going on between us. I am absolutely only here to help if I can. The reason I haven't been at any meals is that I've been working on a thesis in the room, and I'm highly allergic to many regular foods and even have reactions to food if it's prepared in the same kitchen as those I'm allergic to. I bring my own meals whenever I travel. We got a room with a mini-fridge. If you feel you want to come in and see that I'm not lying. Oh, and I'm not sleeping on the floor. I'm sleeping in the bed because Erma can only sleep sitting up since her heart surgery, so she took the chair. Your Aunt Hellen was nice enough to move a bigger chair from the attic yesterday so Erma could be comfortable and not cramped in the chair that came with the room. It was very last minute, and while I am supposed to be here, I'm not registered for the hotel itself." He used the side of his fist to tap his strong chin. "Anything I forgot?"

I stared for a few seconds longer, trying to think of how I wanted to handle this. I could play it off and laugh about his being here and my not knowing. I could also have taken him right to Erma and made her confirm every word of his story. I could check with Aunt Hellen as to why she hadn't told me. In the end, I decided on none of those.

"Well, welcome to The Charmed Inn. I hope you enjoy your stay. If there's anything you need, you can let the front desk know. Have a good day." I left him standing in the hall and figured I'd just come back after I took a quick trek downstairs and grabbed Hellen to verify things without making a big deal out of it.

"That's it?" he said to my retreating back.

I turned to face him again. "What more did you want? A profuse and heartfelt thank you for answering all the questions you think I had? An apology for backing away from someone I was unaware was here when we have so much going on at the inn, and I have every right to know who's here and what they're doing? Especially since we've had a death in the group?" I tucked my arms around my middle. "You could be waiting quite some time before I say any of those things. So, instead, have a good day. Let the front desk know if you need anything."

I turned back around and made my way to the stairs. When he chuckled, I ignored him. I continued down the stairs and then hit the front desk myself. I waited a few minutes until I heard him walk away and then darted back up, hoping to go unnoticed.

Using the key I had never put back at the front desk, I opened the door to Owen's room and then let the door swing wide just in case I was about to surprise anyone. Fortunately, there was no one in there with me, and I breathed a sigh of relief that the window was still locked and intact. I don't know what I would have done if it hadn't been. More than anything, I didn't want Norm showing up again until I had something to give him, and even then, I probably would just walk it over to the police station instead of asking him to come around.

I wished I had something, though, and something I could explain without having to skirt the whole bibliomancer thing and how I had found the info in the first place. I had the same concern with Dean, but he would be easier to get around. Hopefully anyway.

I went back to the piles on the bureau and rifled through them, using my whole hand this time instead of just the side of it. My fingerprints were going to be all over everything once I boxed it all up and moved it downstairs to a closet off the main entryway, so I wasn't concerned about messing anything up at this point.

I just wanted to see if I could find the book.

I closed the door behind me once I was certain there was no one in there who might try to run past me to get out of being seen. I pulled open the closet door and found Owen's suitcase in the bottom, and his clothes hung neatly on the hangers we provided. He had several suits with the jacket hanging over the folded pants and ties around the hook of the hanger. He always had dressed dapperly, and I wondered what he'd be buried in. That felt morbid for just a moment, but then it hit me that he really would be put in a coffin and never seen again. And that was horribly sad.

But I kept the tears at bay by pulling the diary page out of my pocket and waving it near the suits. Something tugged at me, almost like a fishing line with a big fish on the end. I stepped more fully into the closet. No way could it be so easy as to find the book in one of his suit pockets. I was never that lucky.

I wasn't that lucky this time, either. All I found were a couple of pennies in the inside pocket of his purple suit and a feather in the outside pocket of his green suit. There were no other hiding places in here, and it wasn't like he could have shoved it in the wall or something ridiculous like that. I sighed because there was still a pull. I just didn't know what it went to.

And then I was saved by a knock on the door. Well, at first, I did not feel saved. I felt fear race up my spine and then down my arm to make my hand shake. Then I felt irritation if it was the guy who'd come in with Erma. I hadn't been able to get his name from the guest register since he was simply listed as Plus One, and I couldn't find Hellen to ask. I'd have to talk with Erma later about her guest.

But then Dean called out my name, and I drew in a breath. I'd asked Hellen to send him up, and he was here. Time to try out how good of a sidekick he was.

I opened the door a sliver and looked out to make sure it was actually him and no one else was with him. When I was satisfied that he was alone, I yanked the door open, dragged him through, and then shut and locked it behind him.

"Um, okay," he said, giving me a look I couldn't quite decipher, but what looked like a little disbelief peppered with some what are you so scared of?

Unfortunately, I couldn't answer all those questions, so instead, I just jumped into the attempted break-in last night and Norm's stupid handling of things.

"So, with all that going on, I didn't have a lot of time to look into Owen as a person to see if there was anyone out there who might have had it in for him. I don't want to get stuck on it being someone here in the hotel and narrow my vision to the point I could see the killer standing across the street and not realize it, you know?" I asked, knowing that I hadn't done much research at all, or at least nothing that could be verified. And with all that had happened with the necklace and the break-in, I hadn't taken any time to really look Owen up at all. I needed to be pulling my weight on this, but it was going to mostly be weight Dean couldn't see or know about.

"I did find a few things." He handed me a folder filled with actual paper, and it was bulkier than I would have thought for a night's research. I knew I wouldn't have been able to do all this.

"What is it all?"

He took it back and ticked his fingers through it, showing me how there were tabs marked with things like background, enemies, sideways deals, and it was all color-coded. Holy cow, what had I gotten myself into?

"Each section is tagged, and if there's cross-referencing, then I marked that on the divider with the tab. I printed it all out since we don't share a computer, obviously, and sending all of this to you in email felt like some of it might have gotten missed due to the amount." He looked at me with his big gray eyes, and I just wanted to kiss him.

Nope, no, nuh, uh, *no*.

I did hug him, though, and he seemed to be taken off guard. It took him three seconds to put his arms around me. I wasn't letting go just yet, though.

But then I did before it got more awkward. I straightened my shirt and my skirt and stepped back, much like I had earlier with the guy in the hallway, though this was filled with reluctance, and Dean was much better looking than the guy who was way too put together.

"Can you give me the Cliff Notes on the folder while I try to poke around in here? Listen for the doorknob, too. I locked it, but that doesn't mean no one will try to get in."

He looked a little bewildered at first, but then he jumped right into what I was asking for. I appreciated that more than I could say.

I desperately wanted to grab the folder from him and run my fingers over every page, but I was afraid the humming would start again or that things would sparkle, and I wouldn't be able to tell him why I was concentrating so hard on the air right above the paper itself. This magic thing was not for the weak-minded.

"Well, he's been in business for a lot of years. He's had a number of dealings, but not all of them appear to be on the up and up, as he's been in court several times for not delivering the exact thing he promised. But he's always managed to win, so there could be some people who are not happy with him. Then again, he's got pages and pages of glowing reviews for always being able to find whatever someone is looking for."

I began my trek around the room again. I wanted the book, but that also made me nervous about the humming. However, if it hummed and Dean heard it, I'd just pass it off as my own humming in agreement with his assessments. Or I could always send him down for some more hot chocolate like I did in the library. I was open to whatever in an effort to find the book.

I could feel the page vibrating in my pocket. Did that mean I was on the right track? I was standing near the bed, so I bent over to see if there was anything between the mattress and the box spring. As soon as I put my hand between them, Dean was right there, lending his own strength to assist. Unfortunately, that put him right behind me and almost leaning over me. Well, I wouldn't necessarily say it was unfortunate for me since the heat at my back was something that made my toes tingle. So maybe fortunate for me to experience, but unfortunate because I wasn't going to do anything about it except enjoy it for the moment I had it.

I would have cleared my throat if I knew it wouldn't make him move away.

Instead, I let him pick up the mattress and used my slightly shaking hand to feel around on the box spring and then above on the bottom of the mattress to see if I felt any kind of envelope or packet of papers or the book. Now, I could definitely say unfortunately here, since unfortunately there was nothing here and unfortunately that meant Dean could back off as he let the mattress back down to its original position and stepped away.

"Nothing?" he asked.

This time, I did clear my throat. "Nothing. But that doesn't mean there's not something else here. I'm thinking I should have the room cleared out, and then I'll have everything moved to my room and see if there's anything in all his belongings. He'd promised he was bringing that book with him, but why would someone kill him if they got the book? Even if they took it from him, he wouldn't be able to prove it. And if they snuck it out from under his nose, then he wouldn't have known who did it."

"True. The other part of my research is that almost everyone who was middle class and below loved him. It's the people with money he seemed to have issues with. All cases were with wealthy people. He beat them every time. But I don't see any cases involving people with lower incomes. Unless they just didn't know he had bamboozled them, which is possible, I guess."

I had feelings about that and really hoped he hadn't bamboozled a lot of people. "Good words, by the way. Bamboozled, swindled, stiffed. Actually, let's not use that last one."

"Agreed." He closed the folder, and I moved toward the closet. "But this is a lot of people and a ton of motives but no real opportunity. I didn't find anyone he had a problem with who is in this town or staying here this weekend."

"That would have made life a whole lot easier." I opened the door to the closet again and stuck my head in. The clothes were still hanging in there, and a small sparkle flew out of a breast pocket on a gray suit. I hadn't seen that before when I was in here sorting through his bright suits earlier.

"Did you see anything about his nephew at all online? Any connection there? I haven't been able to get ahold of him. As far as I know, that's Owen's only next of kin. Technically, he should be deciding where all this stuff is going to go and how to get it there."

"I didn't look. I'm sorry., I didn't know about the nephew."

Strange that I hadn't told him about the nephew, although not that strange since we'd only talked a little since this thing had started. I had a feeling we needed to sit down and have as full a conversation as I could have when cutting out all the sparkly bits and witchy notions.

I figured we could go do that now. Nothing else was sparkling or humming, even though the page was still vibrating.

"I'm bummed we didn't find a hidden clue or something," I said, leaning against the wall next to the closet. "I feel like there has to be something somewhere here. Someone was making a big effort to break in last night. What was it that they were looking for?" I picked up a throw pillow from one of the chairs in the room, and a spark shot out almost like a full-on firework from the Fourth of July, the kind they launched from the center of the river every year. Dean dropped the folder to cover his ears. That must have been some hum, and when I reached down to grab whatever was sparkling, I had a feeling we were going to be in for a lot of work but also hopefully a lot of answers.

Chapter 15

It was another page. How on earth was I going to explain this to Dean? I dragged it out from under the cushion of the easy chair with equal parts dread and excitement. If this was something that could lead us to the next clue, to find out who had killed Owen, then I was here for it. But the dread part was that I'd have to explain I already had one I hadn't shared and also figure out how to tell him what clues I was getting without telling him where they were coming from. Very much not totally easy. Gah!

Except when I finally had the page in my hand, it was most definitely not a page from the diary, like before. The paper was very new and much thinner, and there was no scrawling handwriting. It was all Times New Roman script. What was in here that would spark the way it had?

"Dear Owen," I read out loud. "It has come to my attention that the deal we brokered is very much in your favor and very little in mine. I believe it is time for us to renegotiate what you want and what I will receive for procuring it for you. I don't think it's necessary to involve anyone else at this time. But make no mistake, that I will make absolutely certain that everyone knows about everything if you don't play ball with me in a far more fair and civilized way. Best wishes on making the right decisions, Caper."

I read it over again silently, and it was no less impactful. Who was this Caper?

"Oh, wait, Caper." My mind nearly exploded on the word. "There was an entry in Owen's bank book about a big payment to someone with the name Caper! Holy cow! I thought it was a business! Or maybe another word for a vacation he took. That's a whole other game if it's actually a person! Now, we need to figure out who Caper is." I glanced up at Dean, and he was seated on the side of the bed, feeling along the floor. For other things we might have missed? Good idea.

"Do you think the whole room has things tucked away here and there? Because it's going to be difficult to track everything if he broke it all up. Although it was his room, so why would he have broken it up in the first place? He would have been the only one with a key." I tapped the letter against the window where the burglar had tried to come in last night. We'd never had a break-in before, so I couldn't imagine Owen really thought that was how he'd lose something here. It had to be because someone – that wolf maybe? – was in the house, and he'd known it. But who was the wolf? I couldn't ask Dean that because I'd have to tell him where I got the term wolf from.

Speaking of Dean, he wasn't answering anything I was saying. "Hey, you okay?"

It took a moment for his head to come back up, but when it did, his face was sheet white.

I hustled over to his side and put my hand on his forehead. "Are you feeling nauseous? Have a headache? Fever? I can't have you falling over on me now, Dean. Is this too much for you? I can do it myself."

He grabbed my wrist at first and then loosened his grip to just encircle it. It reminded me of the historical romances I loved, where seeing the inside of someone's wrist or ankles was like the epitome of sexy, scandalous even.

"Just a little too long bent over. Give me a second. I'll be fine." He smiled, and it did look like his color was coming back, so I'd take him at his word. But I was also going to be keeping an eye on him.

If he was sick, then he needed to go to the doctor, and if he wasn't all in on this and wanted to get out, I was really okay with that. Of course, that would mean I'd have to find my real sidekick, and I wasn't keen on that thought. But I also wasn't going to force him to do things he didn't want to do. That went against pretty much everything I stood for.

He rose from the edge of the bed and his color came back even more. He was looking more Dean and less ghost in the machine.

"You can stop looking at me like that, Roxy." As he chuckled, I listened for if it was real or if he was forcing it. Because if he was forcing it, then I was going to keep talking until he told me what was really wrong.

It sounded just like when we played the Clue game, and he could never seem to win. Of course, that might have something to do with me often having a book next to me and being cagey about using it to help me get the right weapon, room, and culprit. That, of course, was another topic we did not have to explore right now.

"Okay, but you'll tell me if things get too dicey for you. Promise?"

He sighed and then stood tall, and Dean was back, fully. "I will let you know if I get somewhere I can't handle. I promise."

That didn't sound exactly like what I asked for, but I let it go because we had things to go over.

"Do you think Owen brought the envelope with him? Maybe it was mailed, and we can get this Caper's last name and mailing address and then contact him to find out what happened and where he is. What if Owen said no, and this Caper guy came and confronted him, then strangled him with his own bow tie? Should we look him up?"

"No." Short and tense, that one word set me back a step. Dean still looked like Dean, but he had not sounded like the easy-going guy I'd come to know and crush on with that one word. What was going on? I wanted to ask. I really did, but I stopped myself and moved on to the next thing.

"We should get back downstairs and see what anyone knows or has seen." I skirted around him, still not sure what I thought about the way he'd talked to me. Or rather, it hadn't felt like he was talking to me exactly, like he wasn't being mean to me specifically, but instead, he was saying it out to the universe. I'd done that myself a few times, not talking directly to someone but the higher someone. What did the "no" mean then? Was it to all my questions, or did he just think we shouldn't pursue it?

He closed his eyes and then pinched the bridge of his nose.

"Are you sure you don't have a headache? I have some aspirin in the kitchen if you need it. I know you're dealing with a lot of stuff, and I don't want to be a burden. I really am okay if you decide to not help. You love to do maintenance, and this isn't maintenance. I shouldn't be involved either. Norm can figure it out on his own, and honestly, Owen sounds like maybe he was not quite who we thought he was. That doesn't mean he should have been killed or doesn't deserve justice, but you have the ferry season coming up, and I have a whole conference going on that I haven't even been a part of, and it's over twenty-four hours in. I should be concentrating on that, not looking for clues." I walked past him, intent on holding the door open for both of us and then closing and locking it behind me, not to be opened again until the weekend was over and the guests were all gone. This was not one of the rooms that was rented for the next group of people coming in, so there was no rush to get all of Owen's stuff out of here, just yet.

Dean didn't grab my wrist this time. He gently pulled me to a stop by clasping my hand. He touched each of my fingertips while looking at the floor and then brought his gaze up to mine. I wasn't sure what I saw there, but it wasn't the jovial Dean, and it wasn't the helpful Dean. It was a muted version of both of those, and I didn't know what to do with it.

"I'm sorry. When I came up, I meant to tell you what was going on first, but we got sidetracked with stuff, and I let it go until later. But Norm brought me in for questioning. He even came to my house and made me ride in the back of the cop car. He paraded me out the front door in front of all my neighbors. I guess I should just be thankful he didn't make me wear cuffs. He said it wasn't necessary, but if I wouldn't mind letting them drive me to the station, then he'd know I'd get there to answer some questions they had about my movements."

"That jerk!"

He let my fingers go to raise his hand palm up. "The things he was asking were standard questions even if his methods were off. They're looking for a culprit. I get it. People are nervous. I've been stopped a few times when I went to get coffee this morning and when I was in the hardware store with people wanting to know if I knew anything else about what happened. Not because they thought I did it, but because they are all talking with each other in groups in almost every place of business, especially on Main Street. I'm sure that's putting incredible pressure on Norm."

"Well, you're far more understanding than I am because I'm about to go down there and kick him right in his——"

Dean's laugh cut me off from what I wanted to say, but I was happy to hear it. "Always the warrior." He took my fingers again and rubbed his thumb over my knuckles. I had never thought that part of my body could feel electrified, but I had very much been way wrong. I could have sworn I'd accidentally hit the electric fence my Uncle Vince used to have when he was breeding horses back in the day.

If only Dean knew how little of a warrior I was and far more of a bookworm I am.

"Did they let you go because you have nothing they could hold you on?"

"Yes, there is nothing there, and all my time is accounted for even if Norm doesn't like it. I did hear they confirmed Owen was strangled with the bow tie, but they're doing some tests because his bow tie is not messed up at all. They believe it was twisted in a tourniquet. But no matter how high quality it was, it would have been very difficult to use the slider on the extender or whatever that's called to make it tight enough to actually cut off his circulation and breath. I doubt Norm will let me know if they find anything else out, but I'm all in on this investigation thing. I do not want to be pulled in again, and I don't want them to try to pin this on me just because they can't find anyone else. That was the other reason I came here. I wanted to see if you had found anything, too."

"I wish I had more. I'm sorry."

"Don't be sorry. But I do think we need to go down and talk with people either together or individually. Someone has to know something that they're just not sure about, or they don't realize it could be significant. Now, I heard Barney at the pharmacy say he was strangled in front of Mrs. Lincoln's house and then dragged over to the ferry. I'm not sure why they would have wanted him on the ferry except maybe to throw off suspicion. I heard that Mrs. Lincoln thinks she might have seen who did it, but she's not saying anything until she thinks more about it because she doesn't want to be wrong."

Now I felt horrible for making such a fuss about him being here and demanding he help me before he'd had a chance to say anything. And that would totally explain away his sharp "no" since he had information I hadn't let him share. I was not always the best listener, and I knew that.

Still...

"Maybe you should have led with that when you first came in instead of letting me blabber. It might have saved us time." I fanned myself with the letter. "Although maybe then we wouldn't have found this. I'm not sure if it's significant, and I haven't checked the suggestion box yet, so there might be more info in there to see what we have and what we need."

He seemed lost in thought for a moment, so I bumped him with my shoulder. He looked up and smiled. It was a little sad around the edges, but there could be a variety of reasons for that, and my mind was too full of other things to ask.

"Let's head downstairs and see if they're all out of the class with Demetri. Maybe that way we can ask if Norm ever came back with a warrant to look at his stuff, and then we can start at least trying to piece together some of these clues. Although, what are they clues to? I have no idea." And that was frustrating the heck out of me. Why couldn't I just pick up a book and have it tell me all the things? Although I was fully aware that no kind of divination ever really did that. You didn't ask a question, and it gave you a definitive answer. If it did, I would have been playing the stock market and buying lottery tickets every day.

When we arrived downstairs, it was to find everyone streaming out of the library chattering between themselves about the great class and how Demetri always knew what he was looking at, even if the seller didn't. Apparently, he had some stories that wowed people even more than usual. A handy skill to have in his world of course.

I saw the guy from the hallway earlier coming out of the room and stopped in my tracks. It wasn't my conference, so it wasn't like I could tell him he wasn't allowed to attend classes if he hadn't paid, but I already thought he was shady. This just made him shadier. I thought about saying something to the actual coordinator, who happened to be Francine, when she grabbed him by the arm and pulled him aside. He raised a hand to her in an instant reaction, and I was too far away to stop him from landing a blow.

But Erma wasn't.

"What are you doing, Brock? I told you that you could take walks and do touristy things. I did not pay for you to be here for the seminars. If you'd wanted to learn things, then you should have had your mother pay for the entire conference instead of just sticking you with me because she doesn't trust you on your own while she's out of the country."

Do tell...

She grabbed him by the ear, literally by the ear, her gnarled hand grasping his ear lobe and dragging him along behind her to the patio doors. She wrenched those open and dragged him out there, then slammed the doors shut behind her. He didn't look like he'd fought very much, or he knew better than to try, but I knew there was a very easy place to overhear conversations in the back garden. I quickly made my way to the kitchen without alerting anyone to my presence. They had lunch, and I could make an appearance then. I didn't grab Dean's ear, but I did grab his warm, big hand and tugged him along, much nicer than Erma had, I'd have you know.

"What are we--"

I shushed him and banged open the kitchen door where I was not the only one heading for the window high up on the wall that led to the outside. It was used as a vent for the kitchen, and in winter, we closed it to max capacity, but right now, it was balmy outside for a spring day, so it was cracked open.

The kitchen staff were more than welcome to listen in and make lunch just a little bit later than normal, but they needed to move, so I was at the front of the listening gallery.

"I am severely disappointed in you, boy. I have a reputation to uphold in this community, and you're ruining it with your stupidity." Erma's voice moved back and forth under the window, so I assumed she was pacing.

"Is this the part where I'm supposed to look irritated, or were you hoping more for a look of regret? I'll give you whichever you want, but you'd better decide quickly because you have an audience watching from the French doors you just banged shut. And, by the way, do not pull my ear like that again. You could have grabbed onto my elbow."

She grunted. "Regret would be better and suit the purpose that I brought you here for. Were you able to see if Demetri had anything in the cases that would point us in the right direction?"

"You're going to need to yell probably one more time before you go quiet, and I take my punishment, *Auntie*. Your peers are going to think you're soft on me."

"You are supposed to be my nephew, and I'm normally a pretty nice person, so let's not take this too far. Answer the question and make it look like you're apologizing for your bad behavior."

"I'm so sorry. I promise to be a better boy. And no, I didn't see anything in the display cases, but that doesn't mean it's not here somewhere. He could have left it in his van after he put everything away when the police wanted to look in his stuff once they found Owen dead."

"Yes, that was unfortunate."

Unfortunate? That was an understatement if I'd ever heard one. I opened my mouth, and Dean put his hand over my bared teeth, then shook his head at me.

"Well, then, what do we do now?" the supposed nephew asked.

"I know the book is here somewhere. He showed it to me before the conference started when we were out at our cars. He said he was handing it over to Demetri to verify the provenance because his useless nephew couldn't find all the documents."

"And they never found the second book?"

"No, they did not. I need both to be able to find the treasure and then finally get my name on something. Owen was supposed to let me help him with the research and the hunting, but he was being cagey when he got here, and I knew he had changed his mind. And with him dead, I can't know what he did with the papers we signed agreeing to the split." She grunted again and banged something on the wrought iron café table out on the patio.

"So, what's the next step, Auntie?"

"Stop calling me that. We both know you're no relation of mine, and I never would have even brought you here if I had known how useless you are."

"Harsh. Your ex-husband wasn't wrong about that. And if you want him to keep paying those alimony payments, you might want to be a little bit nicer to me. I have chips in this game, too. I'll thank you to remember that."

"There's no way I'll ever forget. We're going back inside, and you're going to act contrite, and then you're going to make yourself scarce. I might have something for you to do later while we're eating dinner this evening. Go get yourself something to eat at the lunch counter in town for now." There was a pause and footsteps on the brick patio. "After you apologize to those inside. You're not getting out of that. Maybe if you're incredibly nice, they won't berate me for bringing an interloper."

The French doors opened and closed, and we, as a group en masse, moved to the television to watch his entrance and hers. We kept the volume low, but it was dead silent in here, and we heard every word.

She strode in, and he walked a little stooped, very contrite looking and as if he was the sorriest of sorries in the world. I knew it was a lie, but I was very interested to see how he played it off.

"I'm so sorry, everyone. I knew I should have kept out, but the subject was just too fascinating, and the delivery was so awesome that I took a chance. One I shouldn't have, and I'm really sorry for. Really sorry." He walked toward the front lobby, giving weak smiles to everyone. No one smiled back at him, and Francine even turned up her nose at him.

"Don't take another step," Demetri said, coming out from the hallway. It was like watching a live soap opera. Where were my bonbons?

Chapter 16

Demetri looked like he was about to blow his stack as he stood huffing in the doorway to the room where he'd taught his class. His normally blue eyes were flashing almost iridescent, but that might have been the lighting. "Where is my gold letter opener? I watched you pick it up, but I never saw you put it back down."

Was he talking to Brock? Everyone was looking at everyone else and shrugging.

Brock took another step, and Demetri was having none of that. "You scoundrel! Do not move! I want my letter opener, or I am going to call the police and have them arrest you. See if you can sweet talk your way out of that infarction."

Brock finally turned around and faced the antique book dealer. "I didn't touch any of your shit, old man. I have no interest in anything you do." He stomped off and out the front door. It was like watching a tennis match. Everybody's gaze swung back to Demetri.

"Erma, you're responsible for that imbecile. We will talk, and I will get my letter opener back, or there will be hell to pay." He, too, turned on his heel and was gone.

What in the living nine rings of hell was going on here? Stealing and killing, and sneaking, and breaking and entering, and people not being who they said they were. It was all very confusing.

"I'll be back," Dean said, and then headed out after Brock. What did he think he was going to be able to do? I had no idea, but I hoped he'd tell me when he finished it. Hopefully, he'd finally have some answers, and we could stop this sleuthing thing and get back to what everyone was actually here for.

And then Glennis came out of the kitchen, and lunch was served.

Instead of hiding away in the library by myself, I actually sat in on this meal. Because everyone was talking around Erma, I made a point to ask her to sit next to me. Today, there were no name cards, so people clustered in the groups they knew better than anyone else. No group was opening up a chair for her, and when she sat down next to me, it was with a dejected look on her face that I wasn't sure how to read. I did know I had to play it off like I hadn't heard her talking with Brock outside the kitchen window. I hoped my acting skills were up to snuff.

"Is Brock from your mom's side or your dad's?" I asked as I passed her the butter dish for her fresh out of the oven roll.

"He's more of an honorary nephew. My best friend from high school knew I needed some help, and so she offered to lend me her caretaker, who I've known since he was little. I don't know why he is behaving so atrociously this weekend. Normally, he's a very sensible and polite young man."

Was that true or part of the backstory they'd made up to explain why he was here in the first place?

"Everyone has moments where they act out of character." Like her. She'd always been a quiet one and pretty manageable as far as guests went. I couldn't recall a time when we'd had any real issues, but this seemed different. Because of the treasure? I had no way of asking, but I was going to watch very closely for an opportunity just in case it came up.

Paddy was holding court down at the other end of the table, but he wasn't saying anything I hadn't already heard. And when I went to the suggestion box after lunch was over, there was nothing in there. So much for theories or help from this group. They were supposed to be big thinkers and have the ability to sift through a story, especially Paddy, who wrote these kinds of books for a living, but there was nothing.

As everyone went into their next session, I decided to take a walk. Maybe I could catch Mrs. Lincoln outside. I didn't blame her for not wanting to make a statement to the police when she wasn't sure, but that didn't mean I couldn't maybe get her to talk to me and just give me her thoughts without having to make it official.

I let Aunt Hellen know where I was going and to keep an eye out for any more mischief, and I texted Dean to let him know I was going for a walk. I wasn't sure what he thought he could accomplish with Brock, but I hoped he would let me know if he found out anything.

Leaving through the back French doors where Erma had dragged Brock outside, I looked around where they'd been standing on the off chance that maybe one of them had dropped something, like the gold letter opener. Although, to be honest, I didn't remember seeing one in the cases Demetri had set up that first night and then taken down when the cops had come around. Part of me wanted to ask Norm if he'd managed to get a warrant, and the other part of me did not want to deal with him at all. That second part won out, as I knew it would. Maybe at another time, but right now, I had a mission, and her name was Mrs. Lincoln, the hard-to-please, never-happy squirrel hater who lived on Front Street.

I girded my loins, or at least strengthened my resolve in my head, and made my way down the hill to the ferry. From there, I'd take a right to her house and please my watch at the same time, by getting in those steps. It always reminded me I wasn't doing enough to make the grade.

I wasn't entirely sure what I'd ask her or how I'd do it, but I felt compelled to go, and being compelled at this point was far better than hanging around and waiting for one of my books to talk to me. It was very strange to have all these new sparkling letters and yet not be able to do what I used to do. I'd picked up any number of books over the last twenty-four hours, and none of them were giving me anything, no matter if I asked the question or someone else did. As much as I scoffed at the basic nature of my gift, at least I had known I could trust it. Now, I wasn't so sure, and I had no idea what had changed or if it would ever go back to the way it was.

As I approached Mrs. Lincoln's house, I was surprised to find the street completely empty. Shouldn't the daily news reporters be out here trying to talk with her and ask her questions about the murder? I knew we weren't a big town, and I wouldn't have expected the television press to come out and hound the older woman based on one death in some long-forgotten area, but to have no one here seemed weird.

She had a little white fence around her whole property, and every other section dipped into a wave and then came back up. Potted plants hung on every post in all colors and varieties, from perennials to annuals. The explosion of color was welcome on this cold day, and I pulled my cardigan a little closer as I opened the gate and walked up her sidewalk. Who knew what kind of reception I would get?

Knocking on the door caused her ten-pound terror - I meant terrier - to take up barking like someone was robbing her and the house was on fire all at the same time. Fortunately, she had a screen door that kept him away from me after she opened the interior door. I had not adequately covered my ankles to deal with the little monster.

"What?" she said, but it was far less a question and more a demand.

"I was just checking on you to see if you're all right. I know there's been a lot going on the last day, and I wasn't sure if you had anyone to check up on you and ask if you feel safe or have concerns." As far as an opening, that didn't sound so bad.

"You never come around here."

Okay, so maybe not so good either. "I walk by here every day at least once, and I wave to you every time I see you outside."

She harrumphed because she knew it was true, and she couldn't figure out how to take offense to that.

"I wasn't outside this time, so why are you knocking on my door?"

Here was my opportunity. Please don't let me mess it up. "I had heard from Dean, you know Dean who comes down here and takes care of the maintenance? Well, Dean was told you might have seen something yesterday that could help with finding the killer."

"And where on God's green earth did he get that idea?"

"Uh… the police told him you had, and they'd brought you in for questioning, but you weren't willing to make any accusations until you were completely sure that what you were saying was true."

"Bull pucky!" She pretty much exploded with the words, which then set the terrier off again.

Should I turn away and not deal with this? Not only was I failing to connect with her, but I had a suspicion that my hearing might be damaged by the ferocity of the tiny dog from hell. On the other hand, I needed to know what she knew or why she would be denying it now.

So, I hung in there, waiting for her to give the dog a treat and tell him to go to his cage.

He snarled at me before trotting off, and I was fine with that since now he was gone, and I was still on the other side of the screen.

"Who said that again?"

I had to step carefully here. "Well, Dean heard something from the police. Also, I have that writer thing happening up on the property, and they were talking about how you said you thought you saw who killed the guy on the ferry but that you weren't willing to point any fingers until you were certain what you saw was what you saw."

"Pssh. Hardly. If I saw something, I would know it, and I would not have any issue with telling anyone who wanted to know. I don't like these lies. Are you trying to get me to admit to something I don't know? I've been around your family for as long as I've been alive. They're usually pretty cagey, but I thought you were different." And then she slammed the door in my face, and her swearing was drowned out by the baying of the hound.

I walked the path back down to the shore and stared out over the river. Soon, it would be teeming with boats and people fishing, and the ferry would be back up and running for the season. I looked forward to that every year, and this year would be no different. But if we couldn't figure out who had killed Owen and keep Dean out of the police's sight, then we were going to have a rocky road there.

What on earth was going on? I felt so disconnected from things, and I felt like there was more going on than the basics. On top of that, I wasn't certain where to go next. If I couldn't get the books to talk to me and I couldn't seem to find anything that helped point me in the right direction, then this would all be futile, and I did not like futile. At all.

Mentally, I pulled my big girl panties up and marched back up the hill to do battle. I would find a book or paper to talk to me, and I would have answers. My gift might not be the best or even the most influential, but by God, I could and would do this.

Of course, that all went out the window when I got back to the inn and found it in an uproar.

Andrew Hemmert, Owen's nephew, was standing in the middle of the lobby with several of the writers circling him. He appeared to be trying to get past them to the front desk, but they weren't letting him.

"Where have you been?" Francine demanded. If I remember correctly, she had been friends with Owen and his nephew for years and knew this man well. With his dark hair and tall stature, he could have just pushed through the crowd if he'd really wanted to, and yet he was standing very still.

"Who would want to kill Owen? Did he really have the book?" Erma demanded. I found it interesting that her question had to do with a conversation that no one was supposed to have heard.

I didn't hear any condolences coming out of any of the people, even though I would have thought at least one person would have felt sorry for him, having lost an important relative.

I decided to be that one person and moved my guests out of the way, as only the owner can do, by clearing my throat and telling them to move it or lose it. I was a little nicer than that, but my tone wasn't.

"I believe we should allow Andrew to take a moment to get his bearings before you all bombard him with questions and demands." I looked at Erma with that last word and then grabbed Andrew's elbow and ushered him to the front desk, where Aunt Hellen was standing with sadness in her eyes.

"I'm so sorry for your loss," she said, gripping his hand across the counter.

So, I wasn't the first, but I'd be the second. "I'm sorry, too. We have always enjoyed having Owen here for this conference, and it breaks my heart that he lost his life here."

"Thank you both," he said quietly. He patted his suit pocket, and I took in how businessy he looked. Not that he usually dressed like Uncle Vince, but he tended to be far more casual than Owen and his purple and green suits with their matching vests. But it almost looked like Andrew had invaded his uncle's closet before coming here. He even vaguely smelled like the woodsy scent Owen had favored.

Hellen came out from behind the counter and stepped into his tall frame for a hug. He bent to accommodate her and then used a handkerchief to dab at his eyes. "It's all so terrible. I had no idea. I was on my way here to finish out the rest of the conference with him when I finally got the call. I'd been in an area with little to no service for the last few days, trying to assess someone's estate, and when I finally got to civilization, my phone about exploded. Do we know what happened? Who did it?"

I had to shake my head, though. I wished I could have told him everything was solved and he could start planning the funeral. Not that he probably wanted to do the funeral planning no matter if the murderer was found or not, but at least with an answer, he wouldn't have to worry about anything else happening.

"Are you staying or just coming in for his things and then going?" I asked. We still had that room, and I'd comp whatever he needed me to.

"I thought I might stay. Would it be possible for me to get Owen's room? I don't mind if it's already been used. Even if he'd laid down for a nap, I might feel closer and get some closure if I could have his room." He turned pleading eyes on me, and my heart broke more. I opened my mouth to answer when Aunt Hellen beat me to it.

"Oh darling, of course, we'd love to accommodate you, but we can't. The cops are still coming in and out of the room, and we don't want them to interrupt your stay. Plus, there are still things that need to be moved about, and the room is covered in dust from the investigation. I have a key for you right here for the room we held just in case you'd be coming out this way." She went back around the counter and pulled the key from the glass case in the wall where all the keys were stored. It was the only remaining one.

"I'd really like …" But he drifted off when Aunt Hellen shook her head "no" again. He had no luggage with him that I could see, so I offered to get it out of his car and have it delivered if he wanted to follow Hellen to the room.

He looked lost and a little disappointed, but I thought Hellen had called it right. Plus, if someone tried to break in again, I did not want him to end up as a casualty.

With him out of the way, I turned back to our intrepid authors. "You might have wanted to give him a little room on this whole thing. He is grieving." I folded my arms over my chest and looked each of them in the eye.

"He's not grieving," Jenny Waite, another author who was usually very introverted, said. "You should see his social media post when he got here. He called it a 'look into his future' and sent it just as he pulled into the driveway. I'm not sure that's someone who's sad his future will include everything Owen owns, supposedly, including the book once someone finds it."

"And the second one," Paddy said, pulling on the collar of his sweater. "Owen posted on a blog last week that he had a line on the other book and thought he'd find it here since this was where the treasure was supposedly lost all those years ago."

Everyone turned to him, and silence reigned in the lobby. "Are you saying he had both books with him and that one of them has a map to an amazing fortune?" Erma said, clasping her hands in front of her. "Why are we all standing around here? Who has waders and a metal detector?"

Chapter 17

You would have thought someone had lit the place on fire. They all tried to get out the door first. Erma's words were like a call to action in an adventure novel. People were pushing each other out of the way, and I wondered where they thought they were going and how they'd get there. As far as I knew, we didn't have any places capable of renting metal detectors, but beyond that, without a map, how would they know where to start?

I stood in the lobby by myself after everyone had left and took a deep breath. So there really was a second book and Owen had thought it was here somewhere. As in here like my inn or just here as in the immediate area? How had he come to that conclusion?

I left the lobby without letting anyone in the building know where I was going. There really wasn't anyone to tell anyway, and Aunt Hellen had gone to the kitchen when everyone else had hightailed it out of the inn, so I didn't have her to check in with either.

I turned to find Dean behind me.

"When did you get back, and what happened with Brock?"

"He slipped away somewhere. I couldn't find him, but he couldn't have gone far, so I'm not too worried about his whereabouts, though I am concerned with what he's doing here."

"I am, too. What's Erma thinking? What kind of deal would they have had, and how did Owen have deals with two different people? We had the Caper person per the letter, and now Erma. Do you think there's anyone else? Was he playing a whole team of people against each other?"

Dean shrugged. "I don't think we're going to know until we can get someone to tell us the actual truth."

I groaned. "And how are we going to do that? You know everyone is always trying to hide things when there's a suspicious death like this."

"Yes. I do." He sounded so serious, but when I looked at him, he had a half-smile on his face and a twinkle in his eye. "We'll go full Hardy Boys on things, I promise. Eventually, Brock will show back up, and we'll ask him how things stand. Plus, I might be able to ask around town."

And that reminded me. "I happened to see Mrs. Lincoln earlier, and she had no idea what I was talking about when I asked about her being questioned by the police. She wanted to know who had told me that because it wasn't true."

His whole body stiffened. "It was information that I confirmed with Norm after hearing about it at the pharmacy. Who's lying?"

Good question. Was it Norm's way of trying to get Dean to confess to something he hadn't done? Or was Mrs. Lincoln being cagey because she really didn't want to answer the question? "I think we might have to put that on the back burner for the moment. We have too many threads and not enough hands to hold them all."

"I don't like this. There's something more here that we're not seeing."

I chuckled. "To be honest, I have no idea about any of this, and I have no path for how to get someone to admit to killing Owen. At all. I really think our best bet might be to go with the Caper angle. I mean, it's the only one that has some concrete oomph behind it at this point."

"You follow that, and I'm going to go back out after Brock."

"Report back, Robin, when you find the culprit."

"Will do, Batman."

"You don't want to go out searching for this fabled treasure?" I asked.

He shook his head and rubbed the back of his neck. "I don't think there really is one. And honestly, with how few places something like that could have been hidden for all these years, I'd be surprised no one had found it before now. What do they expect to find? Some huge trove in a cave? We don't really have those along here. This is not *The Goonies*."

I laughed at his movie reference and tried to think of a way to get rid of him because, with this new information, I wanted to see if I could find a book that might help me on where to go next in my pursuit of Owen's killer. Maybe now that we knew the second book was supposed to be here, it would unlock the other books to finally talk to me. I was tired of only getting the wolf message if I got any message at all.

Before I could come up with something, Dean's cell phone rang. He pulled it out of his back pocket and then stared at it before shutting his eyes and drawing in a breath. Who was calling that he looked defeated before he even answered?

"Got to take this and head home." He smiled, but I had heard the sigh and seen the look on his face. He was playing me with this act, and I wasn't happy about it, but I couldn't exactly call him on it. Plus, that had been what I wanted anyway, so why question how or why I'd gotten it?

"Okay, I'll call later if someone shows up with the hoard of treasure."

He was already on his way out the door, so he waved his phone at me over his shoulder and then went the way of everyone else out the front door.

And as he left, I wondered why I felt lonelier than just alone when he was no longer in the building.

I didn't have time to think about that too much when Demetri stepped into the lobby. "You aren't out hunting for treasure with everyone else?" I asked.

Scoffing, he shot his cuffs and then fixed the tie at his throat. "Imbeciles and amateurs. If there was a treasure, you'd think someone would have found it by now. The islands in the river are right there and not hard to get to. I can't imagine anyone wouldn't have stumbled across something over the past century if there truly was something there to begin with."

"Point taken."

He lingered, and I wasn't sure if he needed something or was just sad no one was trying to buy things from the many cases and set-ups he'd ranged through the sitting room. Which reminded me ... "Did you find your letter opener?"

He scoffed. "No, and I know that Brock person took it, but I don't know why he would have wanted it. It's gold, yes, but not high value." He left with a huff.

Which left me standing in the lobby all by myself with no idea where to go or what to do next.

Back to the library then. Something had to talk to me. I stopped in my room to get a special candle and also to check in with my book of ancestral knowledge and pet Moose. He was twelve, and more often than not, he just liked to lay in the patches of sunlight that cascaded through my window. As long as he wasn't causing trouble, I was fine. After stroking his black coat, I went in search of the sparkle of the diary, but like the times before, it gave me nothing. I didn't actually think it or the candle would help, but it couldn't hurt either, and right now, I just needed a break, even if it was a small one.

I entered the library with some trepidation. What was going on that I couldn't get any of the books to talk to me? As much as I thought my talent of gift was the lowest level out there, I still had always been able to count on it and it felt very wrong not to be able to access anything like I'd lost my best friend and I didn't know where to find her.

I closed my eyes and sent a brief request out to the universe to guide me to something, anything really, to help me move forward. I had Owen's ledger with questions, the fake nephew of Erma, the real nephew of Owen, the almost break-in, and the diary page I'd found in the dumbwaiter that had stopped working, and the Caper letter. What did they all mean, and were they connected?

I wasn't sure why Erma had decided to bring the guy with her, except that he was a total plant and a jerk on top of that. Part of me wanted to drag her aside and ask what she was doing, but the other part of me thought it would do nothing and only shed light on the fact I had been eavesdropping on her. It did require more looking into. It would have made sense to let the cops know I had someone here who was pretending to be someone else, but I had no proof and no idea if it had anything to do with the murder. Just because he wanted to find the book didn't mean he had killed Owen for it, since that meant he then didn't get the book since Erma was still looking for it.

See? Complicated! And I didn't like complicated. I liked easy and straightforward. I liked my ducks not just in a row but also in a chute so they couldn't wander off if they saw something shiny.

This was one of the most turmoil-laden things I'd done in a long time, and I wasn't afraid to admit I was not a fan. Zero out of ten. Do not recommend it.

But that didn't mean I was going to stop looking.

"There has to be something in here that will help me." I trailed my fingers over the spines of the books on the closet shelf and tried to recapture what it had felt like when Dean had heard the humming and the first book had sparkled. It had been a bit hazy and very excited. A thrum in the air that made me know right where to look. How could I recreate that?

I leaned back against the bookshelf and just tried to feel the air around me and center myself. I'd never really done much more than take the fun questions and then do my little parlor trick of being able to open a book and get the answer. It didn't matter which book or what the question was. It only mattered that I heard it and then opened the book. So, was it that no one was asking me questions right now, and I had abandoned the way it once was because I wanted the bigger, sparklier version of my gift and, in turn, turned my back on how it actually worked?

The thought stopped me in my tracks. I immediately went in search of Aunt Hellen. The last time I'd seen her, she was heading toward the kitchen, so I started there.

"We can't serve that, Glennis. That's in horrible taste."

What was this, and how far was I going to have to wade in?

I opened the door and found my kitchen staff standing on opposite sides of the kitchen. Clara and Taylor were on one side, and Glennis was facing off against them as if they were intruders and she was going to defend her things to the very death. She even had a big knife that she was waving around. I strode into the kitchen and stood right between the warring factions. No matter what she had going on, this was still my inn, and Glennis knew a lot but did not make all the decisions.

"What are you doing?" I asked in a voice that did not leave room for going against me.

"I am the head of this kitchen, and I made a congratulations cake for Andrew."

"Tell me you're not congratulating him because he now inherits everything from Owen." It couldn't be that. It had to be something else, or I would have to admit I didn't know Glennis quite as well as I had assumed I did.

"God, no! He just had his first collection of short stories accepted for publication. We always do a congratulations cake for those who make their first sale. I can't have him miss out on the celebration just because some jerk killed his uncle. He should get to celebrate, too."

While she did have a point, and we always celebrated people's first sales, I had to side with the other two. "Glennis, I think it's wonderful, but I'm wondering if we could at least hold off until tomorrow. The cake will be okay in the refrigerator. We'll see if anyone else has anything to celebrate. Then it won't seem as if we're overshadowing the sadness at his uncle's death by the celebration of a publication." Although I wanted to believe she'd just follow my wishes because I was the boss, that was often under some duress because she'd been here far longer than I had been. More often than not, she also felt like she owned this place just as much as I did, or at least the kitchen part.

She put the huge plastic knife that she was going to stab into the cake as decoration on the metal table in front of her and grunted. It wasn't a no, so I wasn't going to mess with that too much.

"Okay, so now I'm looking for Hellen. Has anyone seen her? I need her help with something."

"I can help," Taylor said, raising her hand. "Pick me!"

"Oh, thanks, Taylor. I appreciate your enthusiasm, but I need Aunt Hellen for this, and it's almost dinner time. I'm sure

Glennis needs you here. But thanks for offering." I wasn't sure where to go next for Hellen, but I could just text her and see if she'd meet me in the library instead of trying to chase her all over the inn.

I left them to their dinner prep. I stepped out into the hallway to send the text and then headed back to the library. There was something to be said for going back to the basics, so I sat in one of the fluffiest chairs in the library and decided to start like I used to. It would be so much easier if I had someone with me, but I didn't want to involve anyone I couldn't talk to in the event something did actually happen.

I checked my phone one more time and then set it face down on the end table to concentrate my focus on the book in front of me.

I'd chosen a romance since that seemed to be what the Universe liked the most to make me look things up and then make predictions of things like steamy scenes.

I wiggled my rear end in the chair to get as comfortable as possible, cleared my throat, and closed my eyes.

"What is the weather going to be like today?" I stuck my finger in the book, flipped open the pages, and then stabbed at the text to read it over. "He walked her back to the wall, wanting to do so many things that might be illegal in this state."

I blew out a breath.

"Okay then, not exactly much to work with here. Hot? It's going to be hot today? The weather is going to be wrong for this time of the year, but it will be good?" None of those had the ping I usually got when it came to the right answer, so I closed the book and tried again.

"What should I be watching out for with Andrew here?"

I opened the book again and stuck my finger on a line. "Walking into the kitchen, she turned on the burner and thought about how horribly that last conversation had gone."

I barely stopped myself from throwing the book across the room, mainly because I did not like to be mean to these precious pages just because I was frustrated, but crap!

"I can hear you swearing all the way down the hallway," Uncle Vince said as he strolled into the library. Today's get-up was a pair of navy-blue pants and a shirt that made my eyes hurt. It was still the button-down, but it was a tie-dye with characters from a popular 1950s cartoon character in a bunch of different activities. It had to be new as I was pretty sure I would have remembered seeing it and the headache if I had seen it before.

"Glennis told me you were here and in full agitation state. She doesn't know about the book stuff, which led me to believe you were in some sort of lurch and trying to get things in order without actually doing the work."

He smiled at the end of his statement like he was kidding, but we both knew he wasn't. I often played with my gift, thinking it wasn't worth the real effort. Of course, now that I had decided to double down, I was becoming increasingly frustrated the thing wasn't working like it was supposed to.

"Ask me a question, and let's see what we can find out."

I had wanted Aunt Hellen because she was easier to get to play along with, but if Uncle Vince was willing to be my questioner, then I was going to have to take him up on that.

He pulled a book out of his backpack, and then took a seat across from me and planted his feet on the ground. "First things first, get grounded. I know it works if you wing it. I've seen you do it a thousand times. But let's get intentional and see if you can't get some real information instead of just whether you should bring your umbrella to the park."

I growled a little at that. I wasn't afraid to admit it. But Vince just laughed and then waited while I got myself back in control. What to ask, though? What did I want to know, and how much was I willing to expose myself in asking?

"What should I do about Glennis and her need to control everything in the kitchen lately?"

He closed his eyes, drew in a breath, and then blew it out over the pages of his open book. The paper fluttered back and forth and then landed on an open page. There were no sparkles, and it didn't hum, but Uncle Vince took a minute to look over the text and then pinpointed a line.

"There is some waffling, and she's afraid she might be getting too old and that you'll know it and will ask her to train her replacement. She wants to make sure you know she is worth keeping on since she doesn't have anything on you like she did on your Poobah, so now she's afraid you'll let her go, and she'll have no recourse."

"You got all that from one sentence? Show me the sentence."

"Ah, ah, ah. No peeking. Each person's talent and interpretation come from inside them." He closed the book and put it in his lap. "Now, I'll ask you a question."

"Ask me how to find the killer or who the killer is?" It came out like a question, but I'd wait for him to ask it. I planted my feet on the ground, drew in a deep breath, waited for the questions, and then got completely sidetracked because something was not just throwing off sparkles. It was actually glowing and wiggling up on the second floor. What on earth was this?

Chapter 18

I jumped to my feet and almost flew past Uncle Vince so I wouldn't miss out on whatever was happening behind him. The book glowed even more with every step I took closer. It was burning like a supernova when I reached out my hand. I drew back quickly, afraid it might actually burn me.

"Go ahead and take it," Uncle Vince said from right behind me. "It has a message, and you don't want to miss it."

How did he know so much about all this? He wasn't in my ancestral book of bibliomancers, and I'd never heard him be able to do anything like this. So where had it come from? And why was I worrying about that when I should be grabbing the book before the light went out?

Ah, procrastination and avoidance. Two of my best friends.

I grabbed the book before I could third-guess myself, and it vibrated in my hand like it had all the knowledge in the world just bursting to get out.

"Open it carefully, just a crack at first. It's very excited to meet you, and it might be a little aggressive at first."

Why did I not feel assured by that?

"Are you sure? How do you know this when I've never seen you have the talent?"

"I'll answer your questions later. For right now, let's stick with the last question asked and go from there."

"But you didn't ask a question," I said.

"No, but you did, and this might be the answer."

I slowly opened the book and waited to see what would happen. At first, it was nothing, no sparkly words, no letters forming, not even a place on the page calling my attention more than any other. I was sure it was all a ruse, but then the word Dean rose off the page, and I would absolutely swear my heart stopped.

"No, no, no. This can't be. There's no way Dean killed Owen. He is not capable of that. There are too many other people who would have had a motive. I won't believe this." I slammed the book closed and shoved it onto a short shelf holding flowers and knickknacks.

"Now, Roxy. Don't be so quick. There were other words forming, and you shut them out. Open it back up. There's more message if you'd just be patient."

But I didn't want to be patient, and I most certainly didn't want it to be Dean. He was supposed to be my sidekick, not my murderer, or rather Owen's murderer. Period. End of that story.

"Open the book and start again. Do not shut out what you're about to see. Just take it in and interpret it."

"You do scrying. How do you know about any of this? You're not in my book."

That last part seemed stupid to say, but I couldn't stop myself.

The sigh he let out was huge, far more than I would have expected. "I was supposed to be your mentor."

I waited for more because that deserved an explanation, and I wasn't sure which question to ask first. Why wasn't he? Why hadn't he? Could he be now? Should I have expected the sparkling letters way before now, or was I on track to learning what I should have known all along?

When he didn't say anything else, I stood back and prepared to wait him out until eternity if necessary. Well, not an eternity since I had to find a killer now, but at least for the next few seconds before I started making demands.

"I'm not going to go into the specifics because I don't want to talk about some of it, and some of it is not mine to talk about. But Hellen and I used to mentor together. She handled the emotional part, and I handled the training of the gift. I have some experience in pretty much anything anyone can do or has done over the last three hundred years. But things happened that weren't supposed to, and unfortunately, you paid the price by getting little to no training."

That set me back on my heels or, rather, into my chair. I was not very graceful as I dropped into the leather chair behind me and blew out a breath that would have sent the ferry across the river without a single engine running.

"How far behind in training am I?" I asked quietly. There were a lot of emotions running through me right now, and I wasn't sure which one to grab first and wrangle it to the ground. Irritation? Sadness? Betrayal? Annoyance? Grief? Curiosity?

They were all riding hard for first in line, but instead, I settled on patience. I'd never tried that one before, so maybe it was time.

"Not that far, actually. You've managed to make your way through a lot of the things that I would have taught you by yourself with few mishaps."

"Why didn't you and Hellen train me separately then?"

It was a valid question, and he tugged on his chin for a few seconds. I could almost see the gears whirling in his brain.

"I've been helping on the down-low for quite some time. I give you suggestions and ask how things are going. I bring donuts and check in with you."

I barked out a laugh, and it surprised both of us. Me because it sounded far more derisive than I usually was, especially to my favorite uncle.

"I know I haven't been very good about it, but I have watched you grow, and this next level is something I will definitely walk you through if you're willing to take me on. I still have unresolved issues with your aunt, but when I was here helping with the curse, I realized how much I let slip away, and I want it back."

Did that include Hellen? Did he want her back? Because I had a feeling they used to be more than just a team of mentors. But I let it go at the moment because the book had flopped open on its own, and the letters were rising from the pages without being asked a single thing.

"Call Alberdean and make sure that he and his are okay. Now." I read the words out loud, but they didn't make sense. Who was Alberdean? Oh, my word. Was that Dean's real name? Because, hoo boy, someone had not been nice to him when they named him. Alberdean Manchester? I mean, come on.

And why did the book say I was to check on him, and what did it mean by his? Did the book mean those around him? He was here by himself, as far as I knew. We didn't talk about his family much, or at least not nearly as much as mine. They were all here in and out on any given day. But whenever we did talk about his, he always said he didn't have family. I'd asked over the holidays a few months ago to see if they wanted to celebrate Christmas with us, but he'd said he had no one to invite. Was that not true?

Only one way to find out. If the book was telling me to protect, then I'd better know what I was protecting even if I didn't know how exactly a low-level bibliomancer who ran an inn would know the first thing about protecting anyone. And from what?

I picked up my phone from the table and held it in my hand for a few seconds, not sure what I wanted to say or even how I'd start. It wasn't like I could tell him a book told me I was supposed to check on him and if he could please tell me if he and his were okay so I could move on.

Even for someone who'd been in this world for years, my whole life actually, that felt strange. But there was nothing but to do it. And do it now.

I hit the call button, and it rang three times. I was about to hang up when the ringing stopped, and a young girl said, "I don't know what it is you want, but we're in some serious trouble, and I doubt my car needs a warranty since I am not old enough to drive yet."

I was stopped in my tracks and had no idea what to say to this young child. Who was she, and why did she have Dean's phone? Was she a part of the "his" the book was referencing?

"Um, I'm not calling about any warranties. I thought I'd called Dean."

"Hmmm, are you his girlfriend? Your name came up as Hottie. Is that your name, or did Uncle Dean spell it wrong, and your name is actually Hettie? He's not always good if he doesn't have his glasses on when he types things on his phone. Then he won't change it even when I tell him it has to be right. Words are important. They really are."

Um. That was a lot to take in all at once. I wasn't even sure where to start. I was listed as Hottie? Seriously? My poor brain wanted to focus on that because *wowzers*, but more important-ly, he was an Uncle Dean. How were they in trouble, and why was she here? Not to mention, why did she have his phone, and where was he now?

"My, um, name is not Hettie. My name is Roxy." I thought that was probably a safe way to start the conversation. I wanted to get it out of the way before it became awkward. If she'd called me Hettie enough times, and then I didn't feel right correcting her at a later time when I should have done it from the beginning, I would be uncomfortable.

"Ooh, I bet that means he has a crush on you! Uncle Dean has a crush, a crush, and I'm totally going to mess with him about that. I can't wait for him to get back in the car. Ha ha! He won't know what hit him."

This was fast becoming a runaway train with less than a hundred feet of track before it hit a brick wall.

"Let's start again," I said, and she snickered. "My name is Roxy, and I was looking for Dean. He just left here a few minutes ago. I have a couple of questions for him. Is this his phone number?"

"Boring! But yes, this is his phone. I'm his secretary sometimes when he lets me be. My daddy does, too, as long as the callers are nice people. If they aren't, they have an asterisk thingy in front of their names, and I'm not allowed to pick up those calls anymore because they said very yucky and frightening things to me the last time I talked with them."

Again, so much to take in, and I had no idea what to do with anything I could manage to grasp. What the heck was going on? I did not want to start again and have her go off on another tangent, so I went with the one I'd started before the secretary came in and took over things again.

"Can you get me, Dean, sweetie? I just need to ask him a couple of questions, and then I'll let him get back to you."

"I told you he's not in the car right now, but I can take a message. I know how to do that. I even have a message pad with carbon copies. My dad found it for me at an auction. He says found, but I'm not sure if that's the right word. It was probably stolen, but I still like it, so I'm not giving it back. You can't make me."

Was there any point at which this child would stop going off on all manner of rabbit trails and just give the phone to Dean? But oh, right, he wasn't in the car. So, what to do now? And what about the stolen part? It sounded like she assumed her dad would not have bought her a message book. I got them in bulk for ten for twenty bucks. If she wanted another one, I was sure I could find one to give her. Although that avoided the real issue with the situation.

But that brought me back to the question of what to do now. I didn't want to let her off the phone, but I didn't want to keep her by making small talk when I had a ton of other things I could be doing.

Apparently, I took too long to answer since she heaved a huge sigh and then said, "Listen, Hottie, I can take a message, or you can just call back later. Up to you, but I don't have time to chit-chat if you get my drift. I have a book to read, and you're interrupting me in the most climactic scene yet. I need to find out if Darwin is finally going to come out on top this time. He never seems to win until the very end, but I have faith this time might just be different. It has to be."

It wasn't. If I knew the book she was reading, and I knew books, Darwin never won in the middle of the book, only ever at the end. But the series was great, and there was so much to learn from it that I didn't want to ruin it for her.

Apparently, I again took too long.

"Are you still there? Or did you forget we were talking?"

I had, at first, thought she must have been about six or seven, but from her speech, I was having to reassess that. Was I dealing with a teenager who just happened to have a childish voice?

Maybe I should keep her on the phone until he came back? I didn't have a better plan, so I went with that one.

"Did he go into a store or something? I can just call back if that would be better."

"No, he went into the laundromat because that's where he keeps stuff that he needs to be safe. And you seem nice, so you can keep talking to me. Since I grew up with my uncle and my dad and brother, I don't get to talk to many girls, so I'm good here as long as you're good here. Do you want to discuss the effects of climate change? Tell me what book you last read. Want to share any tips on how to straighten out the adults in your life when you seem to be the adult most times because your dad had never grown up?"

"I ... um ... since my parents were the same, and I still haven't figured it out, I don't think I'd be much help on that last one."

"That's okay. I've been listening to podcasts, and it just seems like later in life, I'll have to deal with some insecurities due to my father, but it looks like most people do okay. I'll just wait it out a little longer. Maybe once I turn thirteen next month, I'll be better equipped to deal with the pain and suffering my family has put me through over the length of my life."

She sounded so flippant that I wasn't sure what to make of her words. Could she be serious, or was she just playing me? Had I called the wrong number and got someone who was both lonely and bored and so decided to keep me on the phone to keep themselves entertained? If I thought a book would give me any help, I would have asked, but that was not in the cards right now.

And again, she got impatient while I worked things out in my brain instead of keeping up my end of the conversation.

"I can go if you're done talking. Small talk really isn't my thing either."

"No, I'm still here, sorry. I was listening to what you were saying and making sure I didn't ruin that wonderful story for you. I guess just take a message that Hottie needs to talk to him as soon as he gets back. It's not an emergency, but it is urgent. Got that?"

"Yep, all written down. Thank you for calling Alberdean Winchester's phone. Please wait for a return call, and if you'd like to partake in our survey, it will come on as soon as I hang up." She laughed at that, and then I stared at my phone screen as she hung up. No survey came on, thankfully, because I was still trying to process everything she'd just said, including the fact that she called her uncle Alberdean Winchester instead of Manchester. Did that mean his actual name was Dean Winchester?

Despite the strange things going on around me, somehow, that possibility caught me harder than anything else, and I laughed and laughed. What kind of freaking world was I living in where the guy I thought I knew and trusted might not even be going by his last name, and his niece felt entirely positive he would call me back once she handed him a message from a book with carbon copies that apparently she carried around, but was definitely stolen because that was just the way her dad was?

What in the hell was happening in this weird world?

Quite honestly, I didn't know whether to wait for that return call or if I should go down to the only laundromat in town and confront Dean/Alberdean and see how many of his people he had with him that I needed to check on. I was going to assume it was no more than the girl and her brother unless her dad was there, too. But the difference between three and four might not be that big.

Uncle Vince cleared his throat next to me and brought me back into the here and now. "So, anything you want to share about what just happened? I can tell you that listening to just your side of the story was both fascinating and incredibly confusing. And watching your face while you were having it makes me think you were probably in the throes of the same thing."

I chuckled because leave it to Uncle Vince to get right to the point of things and break it into one very chewable bite.

I conveyed what had happened to him, and he sat with his hand on his chin and the other swirling through the letters that were still glowing about the page in the book.

"What does it all mean?" he asked as if I might have the answer, which I most certainly did not.

"I have absolutely no idea." But the book had something for us. The letters stopped glowing and then dropped back onto the book in a shower of gold dust. And then they rose again. This time, they came up as black letters with smoke around the edges, like all the pixie dust had been tainted by evil.

"He's back" was all it said, and then it rained down a series of A's and D's.

Chapter 19

"Well, I can honestly say I have never before seen anything like that." Uncle Vince brushed his fingers over the page, and I almost expected him to come away with his fingertips stained in black. But they were clean when he held them up. What on earth was happening here? And yes, I was fully aware I kept asking the same question. But I was also aware we were in some very strange times, and any answers at this point would be better than the nothing I was feeling.

"Wait." I looked toward the door to the library. "If it says he's back, and it rained down all of those letter A's and D's, then do you think whoever is back is the wolf that the other book was talking about? Is A and D after death? Are they initials? What?"

I was up and out of my chair before I said the last word. Uncle Vince was not far behind me as we both raced down the hallway to the lobby, where we found exactly no one standing. But there was a din of conversation from the dining room behind us. When I looked at the grandfather clock in the foyer, I realized dinner had started ten minutes ago. I was missing Glennis's homemade Chicken Parmesan with the noodles she made from flour with an egg, and that was it. She'd lobbied hard for a noodle attachment to her kitchen mixer. I'd held out for a long time, feeling there were other more important things I needed to spend my money on, but eventually, she'd talked me into it, and those noodles were worth every penny. Seriously.

I pulled Uncle Vince to a stop, and we stood on the other side of the pocket doors into the dining room, catching our breath.

"We cannot go in there and start interrogating every person with an A or D in their name," he said. "We have to be smart about this, savvy even."

He was right, and I hated in part that he was right. We had an Andrew who might be at the table. Dean could be the A, the D, or both. We had a Daniel and an Amy who had been coming for three years, and we had a Demetri and an Agnes. It could be any of those people, and I still didn't even know what that person would have done other than come back. Although, I did remember at the last minute that the books had said he's back, not she, which cut out several of the prospective murderers. When had my life turned into using that phrase as if in casual conversation, and it was okay?

I most certainly did not have time to explore that right now. Frankly, I might not want to explore it later if I made it through this in one piece and my mind intact.

The chatter around the table was excited. I was pretty sure no one had taken advantage of any of the other classes that were supposed to have happened today. Neither did they do any writing, which was supposed to be the point of this whole weekend. But they were the ones paying for it, so, ultimately, it wasn't on me what they got out of it.

"I didn't find a single thing, and the guy I talked to down at the dock told me that people have been looking for decades and found nothing, so he thinks it's all just a hoax." Erma sat back with her wine glass held in the air as if she were toasting to nothing. I didn't see her supposed nephew and wondered if she'd sent him to the local watering hole to keep him out of everyone's hair and sight. Or was he still out looking for the treasure? Either could be true, and I wasn't asking.

"It's really very strange." Paddy took up after she sipped her wine and glanced in his direction. "With how many islands there are, it really could be anywhere, and with the way the water rises when the flow comes down, it could have been washed away downstream or even buried at the bottom of the river where you might not even be able to find it on a low-level day." He looked sufficiently pleased with his assessment and glanced over at Dale, who I had forgotten was here. He could be a D, also.

"Well, we didn't find anything, did we, Adele? I don't really think there's anything to be found. And that guy who let us use his metal detector looked mighty pleased with himself when we handed over a hundred in cash and came back with nothing." Shrugging, he took a swift gulp of his soda and looked over at Cathy. What was this, a show and tell day or that one game where the next person has to build off what the last person said?

Francine sniffed. "I went out, but only for a short time. I have stories due and contracts to fulfill. People are waiting for the next installment of my family saga. And no treasure trove that's supposedly been here for a hundred years but never found is going to keep me from paying attention to the people who actually pay my bills."

Erma laughed. "In other words, you couldn't find anyone to loan or lend you their metal detector, and you didn't want to be seen in waders because they're not stylish enough."

Francine scoffed, but she didn't refute what Erma had said. She also didn't look at anyone else at the table. And so it seemed that the conversation regarding metal detecting and fortune finding was over for now.

"Did anyone see Andrew while you were out there? I thought he'd be in for dinner." I said the words nonchalantly, but in reality, I wanted to know where he was and what he was doing. I had a hard time believing he truly had been in a place with little to no cell service. Or that he was unaware of his uncle's death.

I'd seen the social media post that Jenny referenced, and it definitely read like he was sending it with glee. He'd been in a car that looked far newer than the one I'd seen him in the last time he'd been by, and that suit he had on was far classier than his norm. Was it an innocent change that just seemed to coincide with unfolding events? Or was he certain he thought he could get away with it because, supposedly, he was nowhere near here?

The thought of it made me want to go look for him. Where was he, and what was he doing? He hadn't brought in any more luggage, as far as I knew, and even though he'd been assigned another room, I'd seen him outside Owen's room twice already. When he caught sight of me, he'd laid his palm on the door and lowered his head as if in grief, but when I left and then scurried back up the back stairs, he was still standing there. However, he was rattling the locked doorknob instead of grieving and cursing the door instead of touching it with grief. I had his number. I just wasn't sure what I thought the answer would be.

And then there was Brock. He had been hired when Erma had thought she'd made a deal with Owen about the second book. She thought he had backed out of it even though she had been ready to take him to the cleaners anyway. So, what was real, and what was imagined there?

I had no idea and no more time to think about it because Andrew walked in, and two seconds later, Glennis was coming in with his congratulations cake. The candles were lit, and so were the sparklers, an addition I would have preferred not to see due to fire hazard, but they'd burn out soon, and there was nothing I could do until they did. But I'd be doing some things later that evening, like talking to Glennis about her position in the chain of command and how it was very much not at the top.

She studiously avoided my gaze, no matter how many times I tried to signal her. Fine, we'd see how that worked out for her at the end. If she was afraid of being replaced, I could certainly make that happen now, so she didn't have to be afraid anymore.

Of course, I wouldn't really do that because, holy wow, people would be incredibly angry if they had to rely on my food instead of hers. But, oh, the temptation was there to show her there were lines, and she had crossed one or two in the last two days.

I stayed for the beginning of the happy song, but then I left to catch some air. Walking out into the lobby, I was surprised to find Demetri pacing back and forth with the tip of his thumb in his mouth.

"Delivery of your pizza taking too long?" I asked with a chuckle.

He snapped around and looked taken off guard for just a second before his face relaxed back into its normal air of sophistication. He chuckled and brushed his white hair back from his forehead. "No, I would never order pizza when I could have Glennis's amazing food." He sighed. "I'm just nervous about my inventory. I accused that Brock person of taking my letter opener this morning, and he has not yet given it back, and now I was just in the showroom and a book appears to be missing. It's a display only because I sold it last week to a man who has been looking for it for decades. I will have to give back the money if I can't find it. I've always felt safe and secure here before when your grandfather was running things, but this year, things feel awry, and it's concerning."

My stomach rose into my throat. It took everything I had not to gag. That was my biggest nightmare come to life, and I was quick to assure him. "Well, hopefully, it just got misplaced. We can go in and announce it right now. We'll ask if anyone happened to see it, and then I can go check if someone accidentally put it back in the library after looking through it." That felt so weak and completely ineffectual, but it was all I had at the moment. Well, that and the urge to go scream out into the night. My first weekend conference as owner, and I was tanking in all departments. Not my best look, in case you were wondering. Damn.

"I do hope it's here somewhere. I would really rather not make an insurance claim."

I didn't say another word because my brain had kicked in. Technically, the inn was not responsible for any lost or stolen property, which was why he had insurance in the first place. And really, if you had a book that you had sold for a ton of money, which I guess was the case from the way he'd said it the first time, then why on earth would you bring it to a convention outside your store? I didn't have an answer for that one and didn't need it, so I let it go, though it still sat in my stomach like a wrecking ball.

"If you'll excuse me."

"Of course," he said, going back to pacing. "I'll let you know if I need you to look in the library."

"I'll wait to hear from you." I escaped then before he could say anything else.

And that left me in the sitting room by myself and afraid to look at how long it had been since I'd heard from Dean. Or was it Alberdean? That was another one that made me sick to my stomach. Obviously, Dean did not know everything about me. But my stuff was pretty low-key compared to all that little girl had told me in our brief conversation over the phone. Then again, she was twelve, and sometimes twelve-year-olds liked to make things up. It had been long enough at this point that no matter what he had been doing he should have returned to her, and she should have given him her note and kept the carbon copy for herself.

So, why hadn't he called? Was he not at all who he said he was? Mine was just one piece of me. The rest was very real. His was far more than that, and I wasn't sure what to make of it or what I could or could not accept.

As if he knew I had been thinking about him, his name popped up on my phone. I did not have him listed as Hottie, and I wondered if I should. Of course, that would be a completely moot point if it turned out he was nothing like I had thought. That broke my heart with just a thought.

And so it was that I answered the phone cautiously with far less bounce in my voice than I would normally have, and he noticed it.

"We have issues, don't we?"

I did not know how to answer that, so I didn't.

"Let me rephrase that. I'm aware we have issues, and I have answers, but I don't know if you're open to hearing them. I'll respect your answer either way, and I understand if you would rather wait and have me just stay out of your way until things settle down."

Before, my heart was broken, but now, I felt it shatter, and I hated that far more than I realized. "I'm not sure what you want me to say, Dean. Or is it Alberdean?"

He sighed. "It's both. I have never liked my whole name. It sounds very pretentious, and so I just go with Dean because I hate the whole thing."

"And the last name?" I hadn't wanted to ask, but I had to know.

"The last name is more complicated. It is Winchester, but there's issues with it beyond people thinking I'm the real deal that *Supernatural* is based on."

I waited a beat to see if he'd keep explaining, but when he didn't, I waded in. "What does that mean? It's complicated beyond the TV fandom?"

There was another sigh, but this one sounded far heavier. Part of me did not want to force him to tell me whatever he didn't want to say. I wanted to go back to what we were before any of this had happened. I wanted Owen to be alive and everyone to just be running around to their classes, trying to one-up each other, and good-naturedly ribbing each other about who had the better sales numbers and the better launch last year. I wanted Uncle Vince to just be my donut guy, who I avoided his scrying, and Aunt Hellen to not wear a necklace. And I wanted my books to talk to me like they used to, on-demand with vague answers and no glowing letters.

But I knew that wasn't possible. I knew I wasn't able to go back. And I knew that no matter what I did, this was reality, and I had to deal with it.

"Why is it complicated?"

"It is, and I don't know that I can explain it over the phone, but I'm not sure you want me to come over and explain it to you there."

I closed my eyes and thought about the messages I'd received from the books. The one that said he was here as a warning did not happen when Dean was at the house. He was my sidekick, not my nemesis, and no matter what he had done, it couldn't be horrible. This was Dean, no matter what his first name really was or what his last name should have been. This was Dean.

"One more question before I make any decisions."

"Shoot."

"You told me you didn't have any family, but I'm assuming I talked to your niece this afternoon."

"That's complicated too, but the short answer is that my brother hasn't talked to me in ages, and we split ways some time ago. I do talk to my niece and nephew, but I wouldn't have spent Christmas with them because my brother wouldn't have let them. But when I left today because of that phone call, it involved my niece calling me to tell me their father had taken them to the diner down the street. He got them a table and then said he had left something in the car, but then he never came back. And when they went out to check, his car was gone. So, Amelia called me, and I had to come pick them up. He didn't leave them with any clothes, so when you called and talked with her, I was getting them the basics. She had not wanted to leave the car because she was feeling scared, or that's what she told me, but really, she was probably just exhausted."

"Okay. That is complicated. You're right."

"Yeah." He sounded so dejected. I just couldn't let it be this way. Especially not when I had the power to at least make it better, and I was in a place where I couldn't exactly be taken advantage of.

"Meet me here in twenty minutes. You can bring the kids, and they can hang out in the kitchen. We're going to have some honest conversation, and I'd really like you to tell me as much as you can about everything."

"I'll do my best."

I had to admit, at least to myself, that I really couldn't expect anything more, especially when I had no intention of telling him all my secrets, even as I was asking him to tell me all of his.

Chapter 20

Once we hung up, I didn't know what to do with myself. I did a little pacing of my own in the library. And then realized I had offered to let the kids hang out in the kitchen while Dean and I talked but hadn't let Glennis know she was about to have visitors.

Pushing through the door, I came face to face with the very woman I was looking for and also the man I hadn't expected to see.

"Poobah, when did you get here?" He sat at the prep counter with his pipe in his mouth and a frown on his face. He and Glennis had stopped talking as soon as I had entered the kitchen, and I wished that I had listened at the door before I had come crashing through to see what was going on without having to trust that they were going to tell me the truth, the whole truth, and nothing but the truth.

"Seems you have far more going on here than normal, young lady."

There was no real censure in his tone, but I still took it that way and felt like I was doing a horrible job at running the place he'd entrusted to me. That was my first and foremost job, and yet it had fallen to the wayside as I navigated everything else that seemed to be falling apart around me.

I wanted to assure him that I had things under control, but where to start and how much to lie?

In the end, I decided to shoot straight from the hip as much as I could with Glennis in the room. "Things are a little complicated." There was that word again, and I didn't like it now any more than I'd liked it when Dean had used it.

"Things are often complicated. Let's have a snack, and then we'll move over to the library to have a talk. I think there are things you might need to work through, and while I can't fix them for you, I might be able to help by at least listening while you work it out."

"You can do that in here," Glennis said, removing her apron and placing it in the laundry bin. "I'm done for the night, and I'm going to sleep like the dead." She shook her head at herself. "I probably shouldn't have used that word in the middle of everything that's going on, but I'll change it to I'm going to sleep well tonight, and tomorrow is a new day."

I let her go without asking about her keeping the kids. It would have been too much of an ask anyway. And Poobah was here. He could handle a teenager and an almost teenager. He'd been doing it for most of his life.

"We have things to discuss, but I need you here first. Dean is coming over, and he's bringing his niece and nephew."

Poobah squinted at me. "I thought he was pretty much alone in this world, no relatives, no relations, last of his line."

"That's one of the things we're going to discuss."

"Hhmmph."

"Couldn't have said it better myself."

"And how old are these kids, and what am I supposed to do with them?"

"The girl is twelve. My understanding is that the boy is older, but I'm not sure how much. If you could keep them in hot chocolate and maybe a snack or two?"

"And what is that you and Dean are going to be talking about that you can't do in front of those children?"

This was tricky. I didn't want to say anything before I had actual facts straight from the horse's mouth.

"I don't know," I finally said, shrugging. "There are things I thought were true that are not, and some issues Dean has called complicated. I don't want to assume anything, and I'm trying not to spin anything out beyond what I know for a fact until I get more facts."

"That's good enough. Is Hellen around, or did she head to her rooms?"

"I'm not sure where she is. She has her own set of issues."

He squinted at me again. "Issues that are manageable or things that need help?"

Another one where I didn't want to say the wrong things, but at least with this one, I knew some of the concrete information.

"She has a necklace that she got from a secret admirer, except it was cursed, and it was making her fade out and do things she would not want to do. Not anything over the top, but definitely things she didn't understand. She couldn't get it off, and then I had to call Vince to help."

"Vince? You called Vince to come help Hellen with a cursed necklace from a secret admirer?" His voice was sharp enough that I got nervous. Had I done the wrong thing? But then he chuckled and sat back, taking the pipe out of his mouth and tapping the curve on the counter next to him. "Well, isn't that divine..."

I waited for him to come back from his musings, but my phone pinged, and Dean was letting me know they were here.

Time to get this show on the road. Heaven and any other place that rang with positivity, help me.

Normally, Dean would have just come in the door after knocking, but this time, he waited on the front stoop with two kids behind him. He was looking at the ground and had his hand clamped on the back of his neck. The two children who weren't exactly children stood behind him, the boy with his arm around the girl and his chin resting on the top of her head. I wasn't sure what to make of the whole scene, but it definitely cut me deep in my gut. That might have been why my greeting was far more chipper than the circumstances called for.

"Come in, come in, I have all kinds of treats and delights in the kitchen for you. It's a little bit colder out here than it was earlier in the day."

Dean looked up, and there was an emotion swirling in his eyes that I couldn't pinpoint. It felt a little like sadness but was tinged by something very close to combativeness with a pinch of resolve. He was not going to ask for forgiveness for whatever he had to tell me. He might ask for understanding but not forgiveness. I didn't need a book to tell me that.

They entered the inn, and Aunt Hellen was there to swoop the kids into her realm, herding them along to the kitchen and Poobah while Dean and I stared at each other.

"We can talk in the library if that's okay with you. I was going to have Glennis do the hot chocolate again that we missed out on Thursday, but she's about to head out. I've got some sodas in the library, though. It's the only place where I know we won't be overheard." Of course, that wasn't completely true as there was my sitting room or bedroom, but I was not ready to take this into my inner sanctum. The library was the best I could do.

"Sure." He sounded like Dean but a far more muted version of himself. Not that I expected anything different since he had a lot going on and a lot to explain. While I felt bad that I was going to be the one interrogating him when he already looked completely done in, I had to know what was going on. And I'd rather hear it from him, even if he would have rather not told me.

I led the way down the hallway, but I let him go before me into the room. I also waved my hand for him to pick any grouping of furniture he wanted. We had sets of chairs with three feet between, tables with chairs on opposite sides, chairs right up next to each other, and chairs around small coffee tables. I was good with any of them, but I wanted to see what he wanted.

I was very surprised when he chose the two velvety heart-shaped back chairs. They were pretty close together and the ones we had sat in over the last few days. Did it mean anything? I had no idea and no book in hand to even ask. Not that I trusted right now that it would tell me anything anyway.

He stood behind one chair and waited for me to sit before taking the one next to me. I turned so my knee was tucked up onto the chair and leaned back with my arms crossed. I wasn't sure if I should ask questions or just let him tell me whatever he wanted and then ask him to fill in the gaps. I decided the last one was better than the first.

He put his ankle on his opposite knee and then played with the frayed edge of his jeans. He dropped his foot back down to the ground, then leaned forward with his elbows on his knees and his hands clasped between them.

I was not starting this conversation. He needed to.

"So, to start with, I was not expecting to get my niece and nephew. My brother had left with them some time ago, and while I've kept in contact with them, last I heard, they were in the Midwest and my brother was starting over."

"His whole life? New job?"

"New everything. He was supposed to be on the straight and narrow, doing right by the kids and keeping himself out of the trouble he used to get into. I'm not sure what happened, but he dropped the kids, and he said he'll be back, but I'm not sure I can trust that."

"Okay..." I drew out the word because while that was not exactly common, it didn't seem overly complicated, either.

"I don't want to get into all this. Suffice it to say, I have the kids now until he comes back, and I'm not sure when that will be. He left without any info and only some signed consent forms in case they needed to be treated by a doctor. Oh, and then release forms for me to keep them in the homeschooling online that I guess they've been doing."

"Wow, all without any explanation or when he'll be back? Is this normal for him?"

Dean sank back into the chair and cupped his forehead with his laced fingers. "No, not within the last few years. He's been pretty good about doing the right thing. I was glad he had turned his life around, or so I thought, but now I feel they deserve better, and while I might not be able to provide everything, I will certainly provide everything I possibly can."

"I'm sure you will. But what does all this have to do with the things that have been going on around here? And why is your niece convinced the pad she takes messages on is stolen?"

He stared at me long enough for me to feel like I had said something completely wrong. I was about to ask what it could be, but then he blew out a breath.

"My brother's name is Capernicus, but he goes by Caper."

Oh my.

Chapter 21

There had been a few times in my life where I was left speechless – the one time Poobah decided it would be a good idea to put a slip-and-slide down the small slope in the backyard of the inn during a picnic without considering the fact that momentum would take him straight into the black wrought iron gate at the bottom of the hills. He'd nearly knocked himself out with his stunt and had never tried again, no matter how much my cousins asked every summer for five years. He wasn't the only one who didn't give up, but he had that time.

There was also the time when my youngest sister came flying in the house with half her head shaved and the other half a vibrant green right before our annual Christmas photo that my mom liked to send out with her Christmas update letter. There were lots of words flying that day, but none had come out of my mouth because I was the one who had told her to go bold when she asked what hairdo she should get done at the salon. I had not meant quite as bold as she'd gone. I just meant maybe a little more hairspray than normal.

But Caper being Dean's brother? The man who had written the threatening letter to Owen before he was killed. The guy who had received a very large check from Owen, also, and had been on some kind of mission for him that he had thought he wasn't getting paid enough, so he felt the need to start threatening. That guy being Dean's brother and the fact that he'd stood there and not only not told me, but I'd made excuses for his sharp "no" as if I had heard it wrong?

Yeah, that left me speechless.

I stared at his bowed head, waiting for him to look up or say something or do anything, but he didn't. I had no idea where to even start with that and didn't know which question to ask first or which answer to demand. Or did we just turn his brother in? The father of those cute kids downstairs could go to the police, and we could let Norm sort it out.

Wow, if I'd had words, that thought would have stolen them too.

I plopped down into the chair next to Dean and did some meditation breaths. In for five, hold for five, out for five. I hoped this would calm me enough to not have my first words when I found them to come out at full volume.

But what should I say? What could I say? There were so many things. Had he known this Caper was in on this thing? How far in was Caper? Had he killed Owen because he hadn't met his demands? What precisely were those demands, and did Dean know them? Had Dean talked with his brother about any of this before we'd found the note? Or had Dean called him when he recognized his name, and that's why Caper had dropped the kids off to Dean and was now on the run?

See? So many freaking questions, and I had no idea where to start or if I even really wanted to know the answers to some of them or really any of them.

"I'm glad you can slow breathe," he said finally. "I feel like I should be doing the Lamaze breathing I had to do with the kids' mom when Caper didn't show up for either of their deliveries since he was out doing things he shouldn't have been."

I kept quiet because maybe this was going somewhere, and I didn't want to interrupt the train of thought or information. There would be time for me to ask things later. I'd make sure of it.

"He'd never taken anything seriously, and when their mom got locked up, it got better for a little while. I'd had concerns. Like if, she didn't have to take care of them, he would think he didn't have to, either. I tried several times to get him to sign them over to me, but he didn't want to, and they were old enough to want to stay with their dad since they couldn't have their mom. He'd turned things around as far as I knew. Had been doing the right thing, but now I'm afraid I was just hoping and not actually paying attention to the reality."

"I have to ask. Do you think Caper had anything to do with Owen's death?"

"No," he nearly shouted. "No," he said more quietly. "He might not have been the best of people, but I know for absolute certain he has never hurt anyone."

My face must have given me away. My brain was telling me he might believe that, but it didn't make it true. And how had he not hurt anyone by stealing things from them and doing bad things? Just because he had never before hurt anyone physically didn't mean he hadn't hurt anyone.

"I know what you're thinking." He stared off at the ladder running across the wall with all those books. "He has hurt people by stealing from them. He's made people's lives worse by pilfering their accounts, using their credit cards, pawning their possessions, or blackmailing them. But he has never physically harmed anyone. I know that. I also believe he still hasn't. There has to be someone else involved in this."

"He's not here, though? He dropped the kids off after he could have found out Owen was dead, and he ran. That doesn't look good for him."

"I know. I know it looks horrible, but I can't believe he would have killed someone if he was still trying to get him to negotiate."

I wanted to reach out and put a hand on his back to let him know I was there, but I was afraid he would spring out of his chair and stomp off. He kept twitching like he was fighting with everything he had to stay seated.

His hands gripped the arms of the chair, and he flexed his fingers, then grabbed onto the chair like he was going to be lifted away if he didn't hold on tight enough.

"I wanted to start over here and get things going in a way where I would be able to offer a place to either or both of them once they were old enough to leave or if they chose to leave before they were old enough. They need stability, and this new situation makes me think he cannot give it to them. Or rather, he won't. I know he can. He did it for a little while, and it was working, but did he then get caught up in something he couldn't resist, and now here we are?" He stuck his fingers into his short hair, and if he'd had enough length, he probably would have pulled it out. Instead, he clasped his hands around the back of his head and strained against his own hold.

I couldn't stop myself this time. He was hurting, and I couldn't let him think I was cold enough or callous enough to just sit by and watch.

I placed a hand on his shoulder, and when he jerked away, I kept it there, moving with him. I didn't say anything yet because I still wasn't sure what to lead with, but when I needed him, he hugged me, and I had to see if I could help him as he helped me. Since he remained seated, I just kept the hand on his shoulder and waited to see what he'd do next.

And so, I was very ready when he jumped out of his chair. Because I was standing right in front of him, he'd have to go through me to go anywhere. I wrapped my arms around his waist and laid my head on his chest. His heart was racing, and mine probably was too, but his pounded like it wanted to be anywhere but here. I didn't have anyone in my family that I had to deal with that involved this level of trouble, but that didn't mean I couldn't comfort as best I could.

He didn't fight me on the hugging, but it took a good solid minute before he went from ramrod straight to softening, putting his arms around me and his forehead on my shoulder. He was much taller than I was, but as I'd said before, I had a huge personality for being as short as I was.

I held on, and then so did he, and he took some deep breaths and then some more deep breaths.

"I have an idea," I said quietly, my face still against his chest.

"Good, because I'm out of them."

"Call Caper. Ask him to tell you what his part is in this. Tell him we know it's not him who murdered Owen but that you are going to take the fall for it if he doesn't tell us what we need to know. He doesn't have to come in, and he doesn't have to talk to the cops. I don't want to break the Norm…"

He actually laughed at that, and the reverberation through his chest set my entire soul on fire. Down girl.

"So, we call him, or you call him and tell him you are going to care for his kids while he gets his life together. You'd do it for nothing. But for them, you'd like him to tell you what his part was in all this, and then we'll sort the rest out." Had he been on my porch rooftop? Was he the wolf? But that couldn't be because the book had said the wolf was back in the house earlier today, and Caper hadn't been around.

"I don't know if he'll agree to help."

"Well, he certainly won't be able to if we don't ask."

"It's not that simple."

"I live with Hellen and have to deal with Vince and Poobah on a constant basis. I know things that are not easy, and I know that sometimes you have to put them on the spot and make them tell you no, then keep talking until they say yes." His arms were draped over my shoulders now, and he was resting his chin on my head. I was pretty sure I had never enjoyed being short more in my life.

"Persistence."

"I learned it from Poobah himself." I wasn't ready to let go, but I had to, or I might never. I stepped back, and his arms drifted down from my shoulders. He trailed his fingers down my arms and gripped my hands when I stepped back.

"Whatever happens, I'm so sorry that this was brought to your house. You deserve better."

There was an implied "than me" there that I most definitely did not like, especially if I was labeled Hottie in his phone. There were possibilities here that I had not thought were even close to being realistic, and I wasn't willing to lose that on the idea of being the white sheep in a flock of black ones.

"Let's try, and if it comes down to it, we use the kids to guilt him into at least telling us what he knows."

"I know my niece would be up for that. She's got some serious manipulation going on in that tone of hers."

"And it can serve her well in the future if it's directed the right way."

He took his phone out of his back pocket and stared at it for a few seconds before swiping the screen up to open the calling function.

"You can do this," I said.

"I'm not doubting myself, but I am doubting him." He put it on speakerphone and then held it between us.

"I told you I was handling things, and I needed to be left alone until they were done, Dean."

"Hello to you, too," I said, and then was a pause that weighed tons.

"Don't hang up, Caper," Dean said. "I need something from you. I'll keep your kids for now, and I'll do my best, but if you know anything about what's gone down here, then I need you to tell me. They're trying to pin this on me, and I didn't do anything."

"They think you did it?" The voice on the phone asked into the vast library. It didn't exactly bounce off the walls, but he was loud enough.

"They do," I answered. "And you need to help us, or Dean's going to go to jail. Then what will you do with your kids?"

"I'm assuming you're Roxy," he answered. "Dean told me you were hot, but I didn't realize he meant tempered."

I did not look at Dean at all. I wanted to so badly, but I forced myself to stay on topic. "Dean assures me there is no way you would have hurt Owen. I have your letter to him and the ledger with the check you received. I already adore your children, so I don't want any harm to come to them, but we need to know anything and everything you know."

"I don't hear a threat in there. Why should I?"

"I'm not going to threaten you because I don't operate that way, but I am going to appeal to the side of you that's like Dean. It has to be there. I have to know what you know so we can piece together the information we have and figure out who actually did this. I have to have a murderer to hand to the local police, or they're going to build a case against your brother. Tell me that's enough to do the right thing."

"Underhanded."

"Truthful."

"Fine. I was retained by Owen to gather as much info as possible about this treasure he wanted with the book. He had to find it before the family did, or he'd never be able to lay claim to the things that weren't actually his, to begin with."

"Wait, are you saying the book didn't come down through the generations to Owen?"

Caper laughed derisively. "Is that what he was telling everyone? No, it's not his family's anything. He did a job for someone. He was in their library and saw the book, knew what it was, and said he didn't want to charge a large fee. Just that one book would be enough because it reminded him of something his mother used to carry around. All crap, but they had no idea what they had in their library, so they gave it over. Gladly."

"So, he gets the book, and then what?" I asked.

"Well, Hottie, then he started to look around for that treasure. Or rather, he looked around for someone to find that treasure."

I tried not to look at Dean when Caper called me Hottie, but it was hard to miss the way his face flamed red, even out of the corner of my eye.

"I'm going to guess Owen was someone you had worked with before then." Dean did not say it as a question but as a statement, and Caper laughed, but it was sharp.

"He's someone you've worked with too before, so don't go throwing those stones, boy."

The flame of red was different this time, and I did look right at him. He'd worked with Owen before? As in, he knew who he was and pretended as if he didn't. Was I standing next to the person the police really were looking for? I forced myself not to move because I could not be that wrong. I might not have had strong magic, but I had a strong sense of people, and I just could not wrap my head around that everything was a lie from Dean.

"Well, let me rephrase that. He tried to get you to work with him, or even better, I tried to get you to work with him, but you wouldn't do it. Remember that forgery I asked for? The small book of diary entries?"

"I haven't done that in forever, and I had no intention of starting things back up. We agreed to start over again when Lisa went to jail. I've held up my end of the bargain. Why haven't you?"

There was a gusty sigh and then silence for a second. I was not stepping into the middle of that for a hundred million dollars.

"I tried, but when you have no skills on paper and have rarely held a real job except those that were technically just enough to get by on paper, it makes it difficult to have two kids and no real income. I'm only doing easy stuff now, and this one was supposed to be easy."

What exactly defines easy, and how hard would it be to kill someone? At least I had the reassurance that Dean was no longer doing nefarious things, but I wasn't sure how long it was going to take me to square that with who I had thought he was. There were black sheep, and then there were dirty black sheep, and I had some lines I wasn't willing to cross for anyone.

"By easy, you mean you were going to take his money thinking that once you got what he wanted, you'd up the ante to actually give it to him." Dean seemed to know the ins and outs of this, so I didn't ask any more questions.

"Right, so I looked into what was supposed to be the first item, a low-level one, of this treasure, and then I ran it by an associate, and he slipped up when he gasped at the significance. I thought I was on the right track, so I tried to renegotiate with Owen, but he was having none of it. Apparently, he had quite a few people he was supposed to split this bounty with, and he was almost at the point where he'd end up with nothing if he had to pay more. Hence, the forgery I asked you for."

"You said diary?" I asked.

"Good catch there, Hottie. If instead of the treasure, I could find the second diary to match the one page he had, then he could get all kinds of money for it, and then he would be able to afford me. I don't have the contacts to sell that particular kind of item, and it was worth way too much to fence, but if I could get it into his hands and he could let his world know that it might just be for sale, map to the treasure and all, then we could be in business."

"But how were you going to do that without the book? It's said to have a map to the treasure on the river. You don't have the map, do you?" I don't know why I was so fascinated by this whole thing instead of repulsed. I'd deal with that later.

"He doesn't have the map either, and if someone bought it for enough money and then went on their little hunt and didn't find anything, that wouldn't be our fault, or at least not mine. I was willing to take that risk, but my dear brother wasn't. He'd rather clean out sheds, run ferries, and be near you."

Dean snatched up the phone and took it off speaker. He paced away far enough that I couldn't hear Caper, but I'd heard enough, and it was running through my brain at top speed. Who was the person who had been so excited about the second book? If Owen had a page from the second book but didn't have the book, he very much could have gotten away with selling that on the black market. There were people who would have just wanted to own things simply because it meant no one else did. And if Dean was as good at his craft as Caper seemed to be insinuating he was, then that could have been some serious cash.

I made a mental note to see if I could ask Demetri what kind of money that would have brought in at our next meal. Maybe it would lead me to who Caper may have been in cahoots with.

I tapped Dean on the shoulder, and he whipped around. He hadn't said anything once he'd taken Caper off speakerphone, so I had no new information. But I did have a question if he wasn't going to let me listen to their conversation.

"What was the first item?" I asked.

Dean waited for a moment, paying attention to whatever Caper was saying, and then he turned to me. "An ebony walking cane with a sword hidden inside it."

Oh, that was not good.

Chapter 22

My mind was not just racing now. It was going for the mega trifecta of speed, distance, and aggressive concern. Was that the same cane that Poobah had? How long had he had it? He'd given it to Owen, he'd said several years ago. Two years - he'd given it to him two years ago, and he'd asked for it back a number of times. So, had Owen thought he'd find the book here because Poobah had part of the supposed treasure? But how was that even possible?

If my books would talk to me, I would have asked, but I doubted they had any words of wisdom, or even if they did, I probably wouldn't understand it.

"Roxy?" Dean put his hand on my shoulder and leaned in. "Are you okay? I've called your name three times, but you didn't answer."

Third time was supposed to be the charm, but I felt anything but charmed. What a chaotic mess. I needed to think. And to think, I needed to pace. And to pace, I needed Dean out of my way so that he wouldn't see how conflicted I was. But how to get him to leave? I could always fall back on the we need hot chocolate scenario.

"I have a lot to think about, and some things are connecting in my brain. I don't want to say anything until I have a tighter handle on everything running circles in my upstairs. I'm not trying to keep anything from you, but if I try to just spill it all right now, it's not going to make sense." Or I guess I could just blurt out the truth and hope it came across with enough sincerity that he'd believe me.

"I'm going to go get some hot chocolate and check on the kids. It'll give you space. I'll be back. I promise."

He touched my shoulder and then headed out. I allowed myself to dive headlong into the thoughts roiling like a storm about to break.

So, if Poobah had the cane long before this diary was supposedly found by Owen, then that could very well mean that those diaries belonged to my family. Which could be why the letters rose off that page so effortlessly. They were aligned with my bloodline. But if Poobah knew the sword was part of the treasure, then why didn't he ever tell Owen it was a futile adventure to try and get something that was already found? And where was the second diary? Was it here in the house?

I looked up at the thousands of books on the walls and in shelving units throughout the room and wondered if it was right here under my fingertips.

I thought briefly about going along every spine to see if I could find it but then reminded myself it might make far more sense to get Poobah here to explain himself and what he did know. Because ultimately, I still needed to find a killer.

And to find a killer, I had to know who had needed Owen dead or even who would have wanted him dead. I did have to shut off the thoughts of Caper calling me Hottie and how he would know that and Dean's blush several times, but I persevered.

So, there was a book, one Owen had found in someone's library. Which would mean he hadn't found it in ours. It was possible Poobah actually didn't know anything about this, only that he loved his cane, and it had been made a long time ago, per his stories. Could it be a replica of the one that was buried on some island on the Susquehanna? Perhaps.

I whipped my phone out and texted my grandfather. I was aware he didn't like texting, but this one time, he was just going to have to deal because I needed him, and I did not want to talk about this over the phone. He texted back a frowny face and then told me he had the kids to look after and that he'd see me later.

Next, I needed to think about the clues I'd been given from the books. If I was Sherlock, then Dean was my Watson sidekick. I'd kept him close and had gotten far more answers than I would have gotten by myself due to his connection with his brother.

That was a whole other topic I was not yet ready to deal with. I did not expect anyone to be perfect, but I would never have expected Dean to be involved in anything illegal. Not with how kind and straight and narrow he was, but people went through different phases in life, and he had made a choice to better himself then had done that exact thing. I couldn't fault him for that, and I wouldn't.

Now, onto the page of the diary, the attempted burglary, and Owen's untimely death. Had someone wanted the book, knew he had it, and when he wouldn't give it over, they killed him? I wish I knew who the last person he had talked to was.

I called Glennis with my fingers crossed and my heart in my throat.

"I already know what kind of hot chocolate you want and am in the process of making it. Dean was faster than your phone call, missy."

Was she in the kitchen? I had thought I would be waking her up, but this was better. "I'm sorry, Glennis. I was wondering, though, if you could ask Norm something for me. I'm not trying to horn in on his investigation, but I might have information that could help him catch the killer without involving myself at all. Can you call him and ask who the last person Owen talked to was?"

She harrumphed and grumped, but in the end, she did what I had asked her, but through text. And when I got the answer back, I thought I might have a plan that could bring this whole thing to a close.

After Dean and I had our hot chocolate, and I told him about my Owen theory and that Glennis had received an answer that Andrew was the last person to talk to Owen, we'd called it a night and went our separate ways. Tomorrow was the last full day of the writers' conference, and I'd pretty much done nothing as of yet. Although, I was being too hard on myself because there wasn't much I was supposed to be doing anyway. They had everything scheduled down to the wire, and no matter how many times I checked the suggestion box, it was empty. Where were their imaginations? At least they weren't back out with metal detectors.

Poobah met me in my sitting room shortly after Dean had taken the very sugared-up teenager and almost-teenager with him to his studio apartment. I had ideas about that situation, too, but those could wait.

"How long have you had that cane?" I asked as he walked into the room, but before he could sit down. He swung the object in question in a large circle like he was Charlie Chaplin and then sat on the lounge chair and grinned.

"A long time, actually. It was given to me through my grandmother, and you don't get to have it just yet. In fact, I am reconsidering gifting it to you at all since you told on me to

Norm. You're lucky he decided it had nothing to do with his investigation and gave it back to me."

How little Norm knew. "And did your grandmother tell you where it came from?"

"Down through the line, I suppose. She said it was made for her grandfather and had journeyed a lot before it landed here." He opened the thing, pulling the sword out, and swaying the bottom part of the cane next to him, then balanced the sword on his forearm. It shone in the light and glinted like the sparkles I'd seen over and over again with the books.

"How did our family get here, to this town?"

"That's an old question and one you know the answer to. Back generations, our family did good things for the people, and they were gifted with this land to thank them for all their help. There was a homestead, and then it burned down. And when they rebuilt it, they chose to make it a bigger house and sell off a lot of the land. That house was then turned into this inn, and we've run it ever since. Why are you asking all these things?"

I sat back in my chair as Moose jumped into my lap and curled into a ball. I stroked his back and considered what I wanted to say and how I wanted to say it. "Did we travel down the river from somewhere up north?"

"I assume everyone traveled here in some way, but I never thought it was anything but over land ..." He trailed off, and I saw the light come into his eyes. He turned the cane over and over in his hands and then put his ear against it like it was talking to him.

"Is it actually talking to you?" I leaned forward, and Moose jumped down.

"Not talking." He hummed under his breath. "Communicating, though."

"And what is it communicating?"

"Water, lots and lots of water."

"That would be because I am pretty sure we're the family that the diaries belong to, and that cane right there was a part of the so-called lost treasure. Why don't you know that?" I was already leaning forward, but if I could have tipped even more, I would have, except I was afraid of falling off my chair.

"I never asked."

"That's it, you just never asked? Why wouldn't your family have told you? We have books about our powers and books on our ancestors. Why wasn't this mentioned?"

He closed his eyes and seemed to go into a trance. He had about two minutes to spirit walk, and then I was going to yank him back.

"Oh."

"Oh?"

"Oh." He sighed, and there were tears in his eyes. "I hadn't expected that." He raised his gaze to the ceiling and said a very quiet thank you.

"Come on, old man, you can't leave me with one syllable. What's going on?"

"She was running. My grandmother had this as part of her dowry. Her family wanted us to let go of our talents and move into the physical world, denouncing the magic in our blood. She was sent down the river to meet her betrothed, but she never made it because she pulled in here looking for asylum, and my grandfather found her on the shore of the Susquehanna crying and lost. He took her in, and they never spoke of it again. But she always had the cane. She let the boat travel down the river, let it crash and break up on one of the islands, then left a diary in the hull so that people would think she drowned and that the dowry was hidden on the island, therefore wiping her from existence."

"You got that out of a cane?" I asked incredulously.

"No. I've heard the stories about someone in our family, but she was never named. I was always told it was a distant relation, but it makes sense that it was Fionella instead. She was so careful to make sure her hair was always coal black and her face browned by the sun. But there was a picture painted of her as a child with golden hair and porcelain skin that my grandfather kept in his office in a small frame, and every once in a while, I'd coax the story of their meeting out. It was always a little different as if he'd forgotten the details but now, I think he made it all up to hide her and her heritage."

"That would mean that Owen got the diary from the family she should have married into."

"Undoubtedly, and yet we would have the right to the treasure far more than he would have, far more than anyone would since she never married."

"And that means that the book is calling me through my blood. How do I find it if it's here?"

"There are ways, but we'd have to check with Vince. He's the one who knows most of the history and remembers it. That's one of the reasons he and Hellen fell apart." He tipped his head back and looked at the ceiling again. Taking his pipe out of his jacket pocket, he stuck it in his mouth. "I believe we might want to wait on all of that because first, we need to find the killer. The rest of the history has been buried so long that it can wait a few more days until we get the threat taken care of, and we can dive into the rest of it later."

"I have a plan," I said, and then we put our heads together and ironed out the details I hadn't thought all the way through.

First thing in the morning, I greeted everyone as they came down for breakfast and looked into each of their faces. Erma and her supposed nephew were the last to come downstairs, and they barely looked at each other. While I would have loved to hand him over to the police as the culprit, I had a feeling he was not someone who would have had the strength or the stamina to actually do anything, much less kill someone. He wasn't totally off my list, but he fell far down it.

After everyone was seated and eating, I ducked back out into the hallway. I couldn't keep staring at everyone. And Aunt Hellen was in there doing her best to mimic a true devotee of Paddy. I had wondered if he was the killer, but then why would he have done it and when? There was the question of how he'd managed to spell the necklace, though. As far as I knew, he was not of the Mancer bloodline and had no magic, so he had to have had someone else make it for him, but who?

I went back into the dining room to see if I could corner him, but the whole place was empty. I had missed them going to their first class of the day, and it was a day stacked with events, chats, and writing sessions. I wasn't going to be able to keep them from that by asking questions. I'd have to figure something else out.

Clara came in to clear the dishes, and we both jumped when a very loud tune began to play from the floor somewhere. I ducked under the table and found Moose with his back completely up and hissing. The song, though, was coming from the phone next to him, and it sounded very familiar. I picked it up and let it play for a few more seconds in my hand, trying to place the tune, but nothing came to me at first. And then it hit me. It was the same ringtone as had been playing outside the window when the burglar had been trying to break into Owen's room.

Oh, now, that could be a very big problem or just the answer I needed.

I put the phone back on the table because I doubted that I'd be able to do anything with it, and an idea was coming to me that I would need some very serious help with because I was pretty sure I knew who'd done it. I just needed to get them to prove it was them so that I could hand them over to Norm and wash my hands of all this stupidity.

"I do not want to do this," Dean said, sitting at the desk in my front room with his arms crossed and his hands tucked into his armpits. "I really don't."

"I know you don't." I put my hand on his shoulder and tested the strength of his muscles just for a second before I made myself let him go. "But I think we'll be able to get real answers and make the person who killed Owen tip their hand in a way we wouldn't be able to do in a different way. If we just go to Norm with a theory, he might not want to pursue it, or he might ask questions and just give the person a head start to run and never come back."

"You do understand I don't do this anymore, and I don't want to."

I sighed. "Yes, I do, and I promise to never ask you to do something like this again. I'll even make sure you have free hot chocolate for life, and donuts and cookies, whatever you want if you'll just bend a little and make this happen."

"Whatever I want?" Now, he looked at me, and his eyes were intense in a way I hadn't seen before. But then he winked at me and pulled the old paper I'd grabbed from the attic and gripped the quill in his hand. He dipped it in the pot of black ink I had situated at his elbow, and he began to write.

About the move that was going to change a woman's life and how her family was ahead of her on the river, but that was okay because it meant she could spend time working on how she would live with this new life she didn't want, about how she and the small crew were going to take a small side trip at some point before they got to Harrisburg and leave a nest egg for herself that she could come back to. His sister wanted all the money to go to her, but she had managed to squirrel some things away so that this move to her new home would never be forever if she ended up unhappy. If she ever needed to leave him, she could come back and get her things and then make a new life for herself at least a hundred miles away from the family. It would take the sister days and days and train rides to come after her, and she knew she wouldn't leave her seat of power once she had established it.

Dean also wrote of the trials of being a young bride who did not have a mother to guide her and not being sure what her role was supposed to be when there was already a very strong matriarch but that she hoped she loved her husband too much to be willing to walk away from that love just because it was difficult to get along with his family. But his family also wanted her dowry, and she was unwilling to part with that no matter how much his sister wanted her things. The cane from her father, the ring with a hundred diamonds from her mother, the vase brought to her from thousands of miles away when her great-grandfather had been a world traveler and had curated one costly and meaningful souvenir from each country he had visited. It was all hers, and by extension, it would be her husband's but not her sister-in-law's. She'd die on that hill if she had to.

The island they had spied the day before was coming into focus, and she would make a map the next day so she would be able to come back here and pick up all her things when she was ready to start a new life. Two years wasn't too long, and the map would tell her exactly where she needed to go when it was time.

Dean pushed the paper away after he was done and then wouldn't look at it. I felt bad for just a moment, but then I picked up the paper, and it was a work of art, no kidding around. The script was absolutely the same as the page I held next to it. Every loop, every line, every word looked as if it had come from the same hand as the first one.

"You're really very good at this."

"I'm not exactly proud of that, if you couldn't tell. It was what I had to do many years ago, and I don't like going back there."

"Oh." I swallowed hard. I had not thought my way all the way through this before pushing him to do it. If I had something I was incredibly ashamed of in my past and someone forced me to do it again when I'd put it away for good, I would have been devastated. Damn.

I put the paper back down, and while it was still marvelous, I'd burn it if I had to in order to not hurt Dean.

"You know what? We don't have to do this. We're not detectives, and we shouldn't put ourselves in harm's way. We can just hand over our theories to Norm, and he can prove Andrew wanted all his uncle's money and didn't want to share it with anyone. We don't even have to mention your brother or how we came to this conclusion. I'll just say I heard his phone ringing, and it was a distinctive tone like the one outside the window on the night I had the almost intruder. It will be enough to get the ball rolling, at least." My heart sank because we had been so close, but if the snapping wolf was indeed Andrew, then the last thing I wanted to do was put my arm out, waiting for him to bite it.

"No, it's fine. I actually enjoy doing calligraphy-type writing, and this will help. It makes sense because Norm will never be able to make Andrew trip up the way we can. It's not you that I'm upset with. It's my brother for getting himself into these things in general. He promised, and it didn't last."

"He could still pull it out and shake it back off. We won't involve him at all, and if he needs help with money, I have plenty he could do around here, and a little cottage at the back of the property I'd be willing to set him and the kids up in so he doesn't have to worry about paying rent. It'll be like a room and board situation."

He finally lifted his gaze from the paper in front of him and really looked at me for the first time in an hour. "I don't want to take advantage of you. And I can't promise that he would be a good worker or that he'd stay out of trouble. I'm not going to let you put yourself in that kind of situation."

"Let's get something straight here." I stuck my hands on my hips and tapped my foot to get myself to choose my words carefully here. "When I said I was the white sheep in a black sheep family, I was not kidding, and that has not always worked in my favor. I didn't always want to be this way, but I didn't have a choice because there wasn't enough room for all of us to be chaos. My family tree is absolutely stocked to the brim with charlatans and thieves and people who have done whatever it takes to pursue their own happiness, sometimes at the expense of others. Poobah went the police route because it was that or jail, and he knew it. So, we're not perfect here either, and if you have a gift and can use it to help people, then you should celebrate it. Maybe instead of forging, you could use it to create."

And if that wasn't the pot calling the kettle black, then I didn't know what was. My whole body vibrated with those words. My gift might not be something amazing, but it was still mine, and I could use it to the best of my ability and for the best of things and still honor what I'd been given.

Jeez, now was not the time for epiphanies unless they were involved in how to more quickly catch the killer.

I set the thoughts aside and watched Dean's smile bloom from a tiny quirk of his lips to a full-blown grin.

"What? What's so funny?"

"Nothing, it's just that your grandfather was talking to me the other day about how you don't see yourself like you see other people. That you have so much knowledge from books that you don't always see it play out in real life, and I wonder what he'd think about this particular situation."

"If I don't tell on your brother to the police, then you don't tell on me to my grandfather."

I thought that was a fair enough deal, and I was glad he nodded right before the man of the hour walked through the door, using the cane that had started this whole thing.

Chapter 23

The stage was set, and the players were in place. I had no idea if this was actually going to work, but I was definitely going to give it my all. I felt nervous like I had when I'd been Maria in that adaptation of Pinocchio that my elementary school had put on years and years ago. What if I flubbed my lines? What if I missed my mark?

Then, I was just nervous that someone might laugh at me or think I was dumb. Now, I was afraid I might be in way over my head, especially when I spied Andrew out of the corner of my eye as I sat in the backyard with the forged paper. He wasn't very good at sneaking around, just like he hadn't been good at attempting to be a burglar. Who didn't silence their phone when you were making an effort to steal? Even I would have known to do that, and I'd never stolen a thing in my life.

I placed the page on the white wrought iron table under my saucer and took my teacup with me, supposedly to get a refill from Glennis. I walked through the French doors from the patio, ignoring the way Andrew hid behind the trellis of just-budding roses. As soon as I passed through the doors, he darted out, grabbed the page, and then darted back, but not until after he shrieked a little in glee. Fair enough, and thank you so much for falling right in line with my plan.

Now, I just needed to see what he did with the paper. Dean was out front looking like he was watering some plants and ready to follow along behind Andrew if he got in his car. He'd done recon before, and Caper was a block down the road, ready to follow as soon as Dean told him which direction to go.

But Andrew never came out the front door, and his car remained right where it was. Had we miscalculated? Were we wrong, and he just wanted the page and would hide it until after the weekend was over?

I had silenced my own phone for this little play, but I had left it on vibrate to catch any calls with information. It buzzed, and I took it out of my pocket quickly, still in the house looking out the French doors.

"Someone's talking near the dumbwaiter again," Taylor told me quietly. "You're going to want to come hear this."

I disconnected and shoved the phone back into my pocket. I wanted better than the kitchen, where they were busy preparing lunch. I took the back stairs as quickly but as quietly as I possibly could and arrived in time to hear a scuffle.

"I am not handing over this page. You did not follow our plan, and now I'm cutting you out. Owen was already doddering, and it wasn't going to be long until he'd be gone. We agreed to truth-telling serum in that tea Hellen brought him. What did you put in there instead? It had to be a poison. I'm not taking the fall for this."

As far as I could tell, there was no return answer. I had started recording their conversation as soon as I got to the top of the stairs, but if I couldn't get who he was talking to, then it could be anyone, but it was definitely someone who had been staying at my inn and rubbing elbows with my people. The killer had been here the whole time.

"I'm not taking the fall for this either. We're going to do this as calmly as possible. You are going to hand me that page, and I am going to use it to direct us to the treasure. I will fulfill my end of the bargain, and we couldn't just use the truth serum no matter how much you wanted that because he was unwilling to tell us the truth. It made far more sense to take him out of the equation altogether. I had too many questions from that jerk, Caper, and he was trying to gouge me out of any and all profit, so we did it my way instead of your way, and that's just how it worked out. If anyone is to blame, it's going to be Hellen. She's the one who delivered the tea that killed him."

Oh, that was not good, and that was not going to happen. I was a half second away from shoving the door open and nailing Demetri to the wall when I heard another scuffle and then Andrew yelling as he fell down the stairs or was probably pushed.

Downstairs erupted in chaos, and I was left with one decision – open the panel and catch Demetri or let him run and give all the information to Norm and hope he did the right thing to catch this horrible killer.

Yeah, not much of a decision.

I slammed the painting open but was met with a desolate hallway. Where had he gone? There was no other way down except by the stairs, and I couldn't imagine he had been able to do that unless he'd run down after Andrew and then catapulted himself over him like a high-stakes movie and ran out the front door.

Listening for just a second, I tried to get a feel for what people were yelling down below, but it was all about helping Andrew up. Which meant he still had to be up here or on the third floor.

I texted Dean just a name and then went on the hunt. I might not have been the best person to take this on, but I'd be damned before I let him get away.

All the doors along the hallway were closed. I could try knocking, but without a key, I would be barred from entering any of them. I did not want to take the time to go downstairs and grab the master. Oh, I just wanted to scream in frustration and the abject feeling of hopelessness.

I turned to the stairs, not sure what else to do, when I was shoved from behind. I heard the panel close behind me just as I grabbed the stair rail with everything inside me and saved myself from a tumble. If Demetri was in the back staircase, then I knew where he was coming out.

I didn't exactly launch myself over the sprawled Andrew after I ran down the stairs, but it was a close thing. Ignoring everyone as they asked what was going on, I made a beeline for the door to the secret staircase in the kitchen. The stairs were narrow, and you couldn't fly down them like I had the front staircase, so I made it right before Demetri did. I leaned hard against the door and texted Dean to get upstairs to keep him from returning to the scene of his latest crime.

I didn't have much of a plan after that. I should have called Norm, but I really didn't want to. How was I going to keep Demetri from blaming my aunt? I couldn't exactly tell the cops she had been wearing a cursed necklace and took the poisoned cup of tea to him without knowing what she was doing.

Sinking my forehead against the door, I sighed. I knew who, how, and why, but had no way of getting that information to the right people. It could be my word against his. It was entirely possible that Norm would believe Demetri way before he believed me. Damn.

Something thumped hard against the door and rocked me back, just enough for Demetri to bolt into the kitchen and slam into the island. I grabbed a knife and held it at his lower back.

"Do not under any circumstances move. Do you hear me?" I still had Dean's contact information up, so I hit the call button and prayed that he'd answer and then keep the line open.

Demetri had the audacity to laugh. "You think anyone is going to believe you? I'm an art and book dealer. Of course, I'd like to see the diary, but I'm certainly not going to kill someone over it. How absurd." He scoffed, and I jabbed a little harder. Who knew I could be so feisty?

"I told you not to move."

He slid sideways against the counter and then got out from underneath the knife. I hadn't pushed hard enough, I guess.

"We have to come to an agreement here, Roxanne. I'm not going to take the blame for killing Owen. It doesn't have to be Hellen, though she would be the top suspect if it were up to me. How is she going to give Owen poisoned tea?"

My heart stopped in my throat. Did he know about the necklace? My hand practically itched for a book or the original diary page I'd stuck back in my bra. But he was still talking.

"It's your choice if you want it to be Andrew or that horrible Brock. I can make a case for either one. Andrew wanted everything his uncle had, and he was tired of playing second fiddle. Plus, there is a very nice nest egg as well as an insurance policy just waiting for Owen's only remaining relative." He buffed his nails on his suit jacket. "Or we could go with Brock, who is here under false pretenses and using a fake name and is also swindling Erma. Did you know that? Did you find it in the research you have neglected to do while you're running around trying to get books to talk to you?"

Now, my heart dropped from my throat to my stomach, and I felt sick. I clicked the phone off and hoped Dean would not come down to find out why. I had limited time, though, as I could already hear him coming down the second set of stairs. I hastily sank back against the door to keep him from entering.

"I'm willing to go with Brock, though I want them both to pay. Could we do a double team? Andrew knew what to look for and gave the poison to Owen, but Brock was right there to use that gold letter opener you said he stole yesterday as a level to make the bow tie tight enough to strangle him?" That had just come to me. Demetri was setting up Brock yesterday, just in case. So, he'd had three different people who could be the killer, and none of them were him. It was actually very smart, but I was not going to tell him that.

"Nicely done." He smiled, and I had never wanted to smack someone more than I wanted to smack it right off his face. "We go with the double team then. I think that makes far more sense. And the ridiculous cops will have to wade through all the truths and the lies and Brock's background as well as Andrew's. That will take a little time, but that's all I need to gather my things and go."

"You're going to leave? Just like that? You don't have the diary or the treasure."

He cocked an eyebrow at me. "I have the page of the second diary."

Dean pushed on the door behind me, but I put all my weight against it. He probably could have thrust me out of the way, but I was counting on him not wanting to hurt me by shooting me across the kitchen.

"Did you give Paddy the necklace to give Hellen?"

"Ah, yes, yes, I did. Simple enough to take her from fawning to co-conspirator, if I do say so myself. Once I leave, she can remove the thing. Tell her I'm sorry, but it had to be done, and there was no harm in it."

I could hear the blood drumming in my ears like a Viking call to action. Dean pushed again, but I held my ground.

"We have a deal then, Roxy? We both agree that Andrew and Brock were working together in an effort to bring down Owen so that they could get the second diary and the treasure. Owen had the cane but never found the other pieces. I wouldn't be surprised if they're scattered all over the bottom of the river, but I'm willing to look for as long as I have to. It's more than just treasure. There's a magnifying glass, hand carved out of ivory, that matches the cane. Those two things together would set me up for life."

"How are you going to get the cane? Norm has it as evidence."

"You leave that to me. I only need your word that you'll do your very best acting to make sure that Hellen doesn't pay for sins she didn't actually commit, and we'll be clear." He stuck his hand out.

Bad move, very bad move.

I grabbed onto it and then stepped away from the door just as Dean came steaming into the kitchen like a runaway freight train. He collided with Demetri hard enough to send them sailing through the other kitchen door and land right at Norm's feet in the dining room. Perfect.

The last class of the day was just letting out for a writing session, and then we'd have our final dinner for the writers' weekend. All in all, it had gone better than I would have thought when I'd found Owen dead on the deck of the ferry.

I was so ready for a week with no issues and just people out exploring our beautiful area, No more stories, no more murders, and no more lying.

Well, maybe a little bit of lying.

"I think he meant I read too much," I said in answer to Dean's question about what Demetri meant when he said I was trying to get books to talk to me. "I've always loved books, and I often have my nose deep in them. There were a few mysteries that I wondered if I could get them to give me clues about how a murderer could think he could cover up his bad deed. Sleuthing by osmosis." I had to stop talking, or I was going to make him think I was completely unhinged.

I pulled my ham and cheese panini toward me and broke off a piece to shove in my mouth to stop it from running.

"I just find it weird that Paddy would think he'd need to buy Hellen a necklace to make her like him. She was nearly drooling over him the last few days, from what you've said. Why did it have to be more than that?" Leaning back in the heart-backed chair, Dean popped some chips in his mouth and then chewed while contemplating a question I did not have an answer for.

"We'll have to leave that up to unanswered. He decided to go home early, and I don't want to have to talk with him again for at least another year."

"You think they'll come back?"

"Oh, I'm sure of it. I have an article all written up and edited by Francine to tell of their brave heroics and amazing imaginations that gave me all the answers to then give to Norm to sort out. It works for all of them and for me too."

Dean chuckled. "I'd probably better get going. I have to talk with Caper about that house in the back. I didn't get a definite yes, but I didn't get a no either, so he might be in a mood to be convinced."

"We can go look over it if you want. I have some time while they all eat dinner, and my watch is screaming at me that my run down the stairs and holding a knife on a murderer is not enough steps for the day."

We dropped our plates off in the kitchen, where Glennis was on the phone with her sister, telling her what an amazing job Norm had done in solving this mystery right down to the last clue. I let it slide because it was better to not have the spotlight on me and my involvement.

I grabbed my book off the end table and stuck it in my cardigan pocket. I'd asked a question earlier after Norm had left, and

I'd gotten a resounding yes in red, purple, and deep blue letters instead of gold. It reminded me of the colors Uncle Vince had talked about over the water. And I had seen someone new by finally knowing far more about the real Dean than I had before.

I really hoped his brother would turn things around. I'd fallen in love with the kids already when Hellen had told me all about the walk they'd taken, and that Amelia was beside herself with joy that she'd have real women to talk to and said she had so many questions. I had a feeling I'd better always have a book on hand as long as she was here.

I'd flipped the lights onto the cottage from the house and lit up the walkway.

"Wow," Dean said. "I haven't seen it like this before."

"It's usually shut down unless someone specifically asks for it." The last couple had been a few months ago at Christmas.

I used the master key to unlock the door and then opened it, letting Dean precede me. "It'll have to be cleaned, and we might have to figure out some sleeping arrangements, but I think––"

And that was when he kissed me and drew me in slowly, our lips sealed like sneakers to pavement on a hot summer day. I wanted to never move again. He pressed his hands into my back to bring me closer and I didn't need much more prompting than that.

We finally came up for air, and I tried to catch my breath. Holy wow, I had a ton of questions for my books, and I couldn't wait to start asking. But my first question was the most important.

"What was that for?"

He pointed up where there was still mistletoe hanging from the Christmas occupants. "I don't want to anger the Universe by not following in the expected traditions."

And then he kissed me again.

"And what was that for?" I asked breathlessly.

"That one was just for me. Do you want one for you?"

I answered with another kiss of my own until Poobah cleared his throat from behind me.

"We're going to need to talk about this treasure thing. I found out what was wrong with your dumbwaiter." He waved a book at me. "May I present diary two."

And the cascade of sparkles pouring from the book lit the whole backyard in one big burst of the word YES with ten-foot letters.

I was game, with my sidekick along for the ride of our lives.

CHECK OUT THESE OTHER GREAT READS FROM ROWAN PROSE:

Misty Simon, who also writes as Gabby Allan, always wanted to be a storyteller. Today, she has more than 30 titles to date in the romance and mystery genres. She lives with her husband in Central Pennsylvania where she is hard at work on her next novel or three. www.mistysimon.wordpress.com